Dreams can come true with

Jenny
COLGAN

Jenny Colgan is the author of numerous bestselling novels, including *Christmas at the Cupcake Café* and *Little Beach Street Bakery*, which are also published by Sphere. *Meet Me at the Cupcake Café* won the 2012 Melissa Nathan Award for Comedy Romance and was a *Sunday Times* Top Ten bestseller, as was *Welcome to Rosie Hopkins' Sweetshop of Dreams*, which won the RNA Romantic Novel of the Year Award 2013. Jenny is married with three children and lives in Scotland. For more about Jenny, visit her website and her Facebook page, or follow her on Twitter: @jennycolgan.

Also by Jenny Colgan

Amanda's Wedding
Talking to Addison
Looking for Andrew McCarthy
Working Wonders
Do You Remember the First Time?
Where Have All the Boys Gone?
West End Girls
Operation Sunshine
Diamonds Are a Girl's Best Friend
The Good, the Bad and the Dumped
Meet Me at the Cupcake Café
Christmas at the Cupcake Café
Welcome to Rosie Hopkins' Sweetshop of Dreams
Christmas at Rosie Hopkins' Sweetshop
The Christmas Surprise
The Loveliest Chocolate Shop in Paris
Little Beach Street Bakery
Summer at Little Beach Street Bakery
The Little Shop of Happy-Ever-After
Christmas at Little Beach Street Bakery

A Very Distant Shore

Jenny Colgan

sphere

SPHERE

First published in Great Britain in 2017 by Sphere

1 3 5 7 9 10 8 6 4 2

Copyright © Jenny Colgan 2017

The moral right of the author has been asserted.

A CIP catalogue record for this book
is available from the British Library.

ISBN 978-0-7515-6619-2

Typeset in Stone Serif by M Rules
Printed and bound in Great Britain by
Clays Ltd, St Ives plc

Papers used by Sphere are from well-managed forests
and other responsible sources.

MIX
Paper from
responsible sources
FSC® C104740

Sphere
An imprint of
Little, Brown Book Group
Carmelite House
50 Victoria Embankment
London EC4Y 0DZ

An Hachette UK Company
www.hachette.co.uk

www.littlebrown.co.uk

Chapter 1

'Name?'

'I told you,' said the man. 'I have told you many times.'

There was, Saif knew, no point in getting angry or impatient. If you did, you got sent to the back of the queue, and that meant another night outdoors. Although spring was coming soon, it wasn't here yet.

The cold seemed to have settled in his bones; he couldn't remember what it felt like to be warm – properly warm.

'Saif Hassan. From Damascus.'

'What school did you go to? What was the mayor's name? What is the main shopping street called?'

All of these questions were meant to catch him out, to trip him up, to root out the unlucky but hopeful Somalis and Tunisians. He'd even met a man from Haiti, perhaps the least likely refugee from a Middle Eastern war he'd ever seen. There were others, from countries he'd

1

barely heard of – and he knew a bit about the world.

He answered the questions again and again, as the boys behind him in the queue whispered to one another, 'What did he say? What is he asking? Write it down.' He stood patiently and waited, clutching his black bag, the only thing he'd been able to save from the boat.

The only thing.

Chapter 2

Lorna was late again. She switched off the car radio with its news of yet more terrible things going on in the world. She knew there were far worse things happening than her being late, but at the moment that didn't really help.

'Come on, Dad,' she said, getting out the car. She held the old man's arm as he slowly pulled himself out. She looked nervously at her watch. She was definitely going to be late. Her heart sank as she saw there was already a queue in front of the surgery.

The wind clipped in from the west, causing one or two drops of what felt like hail. Please, no. Not a hailstorm. Making a seventy-four-year-old man with a migraine wait in a spring hailstorm really was just not fair. But there was a long queue to see the last remaining doctor on the remote Scottish island of Mure.

'Just leave me,' he muttered, as he always did.

'Don't be daft,' said Lorna. Angus didn't hear half as well as he pretended he did; he'd never hear what the doctor told him. And she couldn't trust what time they would see him, if they did at all. There were at least ten people in front of them: mothers with wailing children; old biddies who looked as if they were having a bit of a day out; workers looking miserable as they stared at their phones.

'It might take a while,' she said. 'But I'll get you in and settled.'

That meant missing the infants' assembly. Mrs Cook would have to do it. But Lorna knew that the very littlest in the school – and their parents – liked it a lot more when the headmistress was there. She could have yelled with frustration. She pushed her curly auburn hair crossly behind her ears.

'There was only one doctor here when I was a lad,' said Angus.

'Yes, but there were a lot fewer people when you were a lad,' said Lorna. 'And they all got killed by farm machinery or just lay down and died at fifty-five. Doctors weren't quite so in demand.'

'Yes, well,' said Angus. 'It was a Dr MacAllister then too – the young doctor. Although he wasn't that young. He took over from his father, old Dr MacAllister, who took over from *his* father—'

'Who used leeches,' said Lorna crossly. She

glanced at her watch. She was friendly with Jeannie, the receptionist, but that didn't help. She wouldn't do her a favour. And no way would Jeannie open up that metal shutter until 8.30 a.m. precisely.

'You need to be getting on, love,' said her father as she glanced at her watch again.

'No, Dad,' she said, feeling annoyed with herself for being grumpy. 'It's fine.'

She thought with some concern about the school roll for next year. It was down again. The problem was that they couldn't get a new doctor, so people didn't want to move here. They'd rather go to Orkney, or somewhere else with a lot going on, or just stay in Glasgow. It was bad all round.

Everyone knew that the GP position had been advertised for eight months now without a single applicant. It was the same everywhere. A huge shortage of doctors all over the country, and very few that wanted to bring their much-needed skills to an island this small and out of the way.

She sighed as Jeannie arrived and made a big show of unlocking and rolling up the shutter. It was 8.30 exactly.

The queue, which several people had joined since they'd got there, surged forward. Lorna thought, a little unkindly, that anyone who could push to the front of a queue probably didn't need to be at the doctor's at all. She followed the rest, still holding her dad's arm, into the welcoming warmth of the overheated waiting room.

Chapter 3

Saif knew there were too many refugees in the queue waiting to be seen in the barn by the great barbed-wire fence. The crowd had also realised that there were too many for them all to be seen today, and people were pushing and shoving.

Saif knew better than to go anywhere near that. He was tall and stood out. He was older than many of the men, but his build could attract aggression. All he wanted to do was stay out of trouble. He'd seen enough for a lifetime.

This, though, was getting nasty. The officials behind the fence seemed for the moment to have disappeared, and there was jostling and raised voices from the back of the crowd. He caught the eye of a very young woman with a quiet – scarily quiet – baby in a tattered old buggy, and they both looked away. No more trouble. Please.

It happened very quickly. Just shouts, really. That was all. Then a woman's scream rang out, and instantly a clutch of heavily armed guards came through the barn door. They came as if from nowhere, one still chewing, batons raised, hands on their guns. The space immediately went dead silent. The men rushed apart, heads bowed, like naughty schoolboys discovered behaving badly when the teacher was out of the classroom.

But the woman's voice wailed on. Heads that had stiffened, staring at the floor, desperate not to attract attention, began to look around a little.

The man in charge of the guards said something in his own language that was patently a curse. Saif took a quick look.

The woman was cradling a child in her arms, a small boy of not much more than seven or eight. He wasn't crying out, which worried Saif, but his eyes were wide with fear, his skin pale. Blood was spurting from a wound on his shoulder. Obviously one of the young men had had a knife, and something had gone terribly wrong.

The crowd cleared to give the woman space. The commander spoke into his walkie-talkie, but obviously got a reply he did not like. He looked around, shouting the word in different languages: 'Doctor? *Médecin? Tabib?*'

Again, everyone stared at the floor. Saif heaved a sigh. It was not the first time, and it would not be the last. He raised his hand.

'Yes,' he said quietly.

Chapter 4

'Well, when can I have an appointment? He's had that head for three weeks. He just can't shift it.'

'Lorna, you know I'm doing my best,' said Jeannie, staring at the computer. It was as if, if she clicked on it enough, Dr MacAllister's time would magically expand and new slots would open up. He should have retired a while ago. They all knew it. But until they got a new doctor he couldn't bring himself to leave his post. In fact, they needed two new doctors. You couldn't run the island single-handed; it was ridiculous.

The old doctor staying on was honourable, of course, but not at all practical. He was tired. He was getting more tired. House calls were more difficult all the time, and he couldn't manage computers. He had never learned, which meant that Jeannie spent long hours of unpaid overtime trying to get the records straight. And as tests were sent by boat to the mainland, they had to wait for the weather, sometimes, to get the results back.

Jeannie and the doctor were clinging on by their fingernails, and they both knew it. Sandy MacAllister had started taking an extra tot of whisky when he got home at night, even though he knew it was making things worse than ever. His wife was in despair. They'd raised three strapping sons on the island, clever, strong boys, their parents' pride and joy. One was a dentist in Edinburgh, one was at medical school in Cambridge, and one was vaccinating children in Africa for the Red Cross. None of that did the island of Mure much good.

Jeannie glanced up at her friend.

'Leave him,' she said. 'But don't tell the others. I don't want any granny-dumping in my surgery.'

'But you—'

'I'll figure something out. Sandy will talk to me. I'll write it all down for you.'

'Jeannie, you are one in a million.'

'DON'T tell the others.'

Jeannie turned to the next in line, poor hopeless Wullie MacIver, whose three talents – washing windows, taxi-driving and drinking cider – served him very badly.

'What is it this time, Wullie?'

10

'Hairline fracture?' said Wullie hopefully. 'Might be a bad sprain, yes.'

They both looked down at his very naked, very dirty foot. It was huge, swollen and a rather deep shade of purple.

'See you later,' said Jeannie to Lorna, who, full of gratitude, sat her dad down with a *Farmers Weekly* and told him that everything would be all right. She dashed out of the door.

Chapter 5

All eyes were on Saif as he walked forward, his black bag clasped firmly in his hand.

'Camp doctor is busy,' said the commander, eyeing him carefully. 'Are you a real doctor? We get a lot of not-real doctors. They say doctor to get a passport.'

Once upon a time, this kind of thing would have made Saif angry. No longer. He simply opened up his bag, with its stethoscope, the tattered old blood pressure cuff, and the few bandages he had left. The commander nodded as he crouched down.

'This is your boy?' Saif said in Arabic to the woman, who, terrified, nodded silently back.

'What's his name?' He looked at the child. 'What's your name?'

'Medhi,' muttered the little boy, his eyes wide, his body shaking. 'It hurts! It hurts! It hurts!'

'I know,' said Saif. 'I know that. I'm going to take a look at it, okay? Just take a look. I promise I won't do anything without telling you.'

He pulled out his scissors – Medhi watched him anxiously – and gently cut around the cloth on the shoulder. He could tell by the worried noise the mother made that these were the only clothes the boy had, but they were now soaked with blood.

As he carefully removed the shreds of material from the wound, Medhi groaned. Tears were running down his face. He had learned, somewhere, somehow, to remain very, very quiet. Saif didn't want to think how.

The wound was deep, and still bleeding heavily. Saif glanced around the silent room. In one corner sat a young man. He was thin but muscular, wearing a filthy old shell suit. He had three days' growth of beard on his face. He was trying to look grown up but he was truly no more than a boy himself. He was shaking and quietly crying. Saif stared at him until the man was in no doubt that he'd been spotted. Then Saif returned to his work.

'I'll need alcohol,' he said to the guard. 'Drugs if you have them.'

'I thought you Muslims didn't drink,' said the man in charge. 'Drugs too, huh?'

His comrades laughed, even those who probably didn't speak English. It was safest to go along with the big man.

13

'To sterilise the wound,' said Saif. He ignored the joke. Never listen. Never respond. 'And if you have some painkillers, that too would be helpful.'

Rubbing alcohol was brought as Saif tried to staunch the flow of blood; there was no place to put a tourniquet. But nothing stronger than paracetamol could be found in the camp. The other drugs had been stolen, Saif supposed.

He looked at the boy's mother, wondering if she understood what needed to be done.

'I'm going to have to stitch him,' he said.

Instantly the woman's mouth grew wide and she started wailing again. The boy turned his head in a panic.

'You must stay calm,' Saif said, but she couldn't.

Everyone here had been through great hardship. Great peril, great trials. But everyone had a breaking point, and this was hers. She yelled, and waved her arms to protect her boy, and the other women gathered around her. They formed a protective ring, holding her in a safe circle of female flesh.

'Don't worry, Medhi,' said Saif, as calmly as he could. 'I'm going to do something to make you better. It's going to hurt. But after that it won't hurt and it will get better.'

'Are you going to cut off my arm with those scissors?' said the boy.

'No, of course not,' said Saif. The boy's face relaxed a little, and Saif's heart sank as he thought of what he was about to do. There was no other way to stop the bleeding.

'I need three men,' he said. When nobody came forward, he picked the two largest men he could see. 'And you,' he added, nodding to the shaking teen in the corner. The young man would sit and endure the child's pain. If that could not teach him, nothing would.

The men were each given a limb to hold. Medhi's face was now a mask of terror. But Saif would not cover up his mouth; he couldn't risk him suffocating. As long as the boy was screaming, he knew that he was still all right.

Offering a quick prayer, he went to the corner of the barn and began to scrub his hands.

Chapter 6

The hail had, thankfully, stopped as Lorna hopped back in her beloved little Mini and took off up the breezy main street. As so often at this time of year, all four seasons had come to Mure in the space of half an hour. Bent by the wind, snowdrops poked their sturdy heads through the soil; crocuses burst up all over.

Lorna drove along the seafront, slowing, although she was late, to watch a heron make a perfect landing by the water. She turned left up the hill, finally reaching her place of work.

The school was almost as old as the parish itself. Its grey floors were softened and crumbled by generations of little Mure feet, even as the number of pupils had risen and fallen through hard times, and emigration, and wars. The building was warm in the winter, when many of its pupils' homes were cold; empty in the autumn if the harvest was late; packed full at Christmas time.

She marched through the now-empty

playground, smiling at another straggler, who looked at her with fear in his face and muttered, 'Good MORNING, Miss Lorna.'

'On with you, Ranald MacRanald,' she said, and he scuttled inside on plump, freckled legs.

The assembly was nearly over. There were six children in Primary 1. It didn't matter how many times she counted them, it wasn't enough. And she knew that little Heather Skinner had just been diagnosed with type 1 diabetes. It was a tragedy for the family, obviously, but a tragedy for the island too. They were a fairly new family, the Skinners; he worked on the oil rigs and wanted somewhere safe and comfortable for his young family to grow up. But they wouldn't be able to stay here, because they needed a hospital.

She headed into her tiny, untidy office. As usual, snotty Malcolm from Primary 6 was waiting outside for her, having caused trouble somewhere or other. Malcolm was barely ten, but already he had the broad shoulders and hefty build of generations of Mure men who were used to throwing cows about. He had not the slightest use for school, and she often felt she agreed with him. Nothing she could do or say did any good. He was desperate to be suspended so he could join his big brothers working in the fields, patching up old motorbikes and spending their modest wages down the pub. She simply nodded and decided to deal with him shortly.

The form was on her desk, buried under various Curriculum for Excellence pieces of paper. People thought it was easy running a very small school, but you got just as much government paperwork as everybody else, without half as much help. She pulled the form out anyway. It was from the local council and was headed 'Application for Emergency Medical Care Forms B2/75'. It needed a back-up letter from a 'respected member of the community', which seemed to mean her, the spinster headmistress. She sighed. She was only thirty, but people married early round here.

She opened her creaky, ancient computer and began to type a letter to her MP.

Chapter 7

Saif couldn't have told you afterwards how long
he had worked, although he went as quickly as
he safely could. Everything became a dream of
concentration: the sweat on Medhi's skin and how
he tried so hard to stop himself from shouting
out; the crying teenager holding the boy's legs,
praying under his breath for forgiveness; the
hush in the great processing barn, except for the
odd sob from the child's mother.

He didn't notice the man arrive until he had
finished, with sweat on his own brow but his
work done, nimble and quick. Then he looked
up and saw the man staring at him.

He wasn't local; you could tell that by the suit,
which was unusual. Saif knew somehow that it
was expensive. He was very tall and thin and
pale, and surrounded by young, keen-looking
people – from the charities and voluntary
groups, Saif supposed. He had met many of
them on the way. Their help was limited and
sometimes confusing.

Anyway, he ignored him and tried to talk to the boy's mother, who was now sobbing and clutching his arm. Her other arm was round the boy, who was lying against her, falling into a feverish sleep. He told her that it was important to keep the wound clean, to disinfect it, to give her boy medicine if she could get hold of it.

Then he turned to the crying teenager and stared him straight in the eye.

'Give me the knife,' he said quietly. The boy, still shaking, handed it over without arguing. 'We have to do this peacefully or not at all, God willing,' Saif said, putting it in his bag. It might yet come in useful.

Someone cleared his throat. It was the tall, pale man he had noticed before.

'You speak English?' said the man in a clipped voice.

Saif nodded. 'I have English qualifications.'

They paused at that. He'd been saying it at every border for so long, and no one had cared. But now they looked at one another.

'Follow me.'

Saif glanced behind him at the boy. He still didn't like his colour, or the drowsiness in his eyes. The woman stared at him. But there was nothing more he could do.

*

20

'There is a place for you. Do you understand what I am saying?'

The man was talking, but Saif was so tired he could barely make out what he was saying. It was as if all his energy had been saved for travelling, for staying alert and out of people's way. And now that he had been found, now that someone was paying him some attention, the tiredness, the tension, needed to release itself. He could hardly keep his eyes open.

He blinked. Now was not the time to lose concentration.

'What about my family?' he asked. The tall man looked mildly annoyed, as if a family was a tedious pest, like lice.

'Where are they?'

'We got . . . separated. In . . . '

He couldn't think about that night. The cold, the flashing, the panic. The no way of knowing which way was up. The shouting, in so many different languages. No. He couldn't think about it. He forced himself to speak nicely. His father had been a language professor at the university, a noisy, energetic man of the world. He had rather overshadowed his youngest son, and had forced Saif to take the British exams at the University of Beirut. 'Then you can work anywhere,' he had said, as Saif struggled with English spelling.

It had, Saif knew, broken his father's heart when he'd chosen to go back to Syria, the country of his birth, and work for the poor of Damascus. His father had had bigger dreams than that. He had seen how things might turn out.

Saif missed him every day.

'On a boat,' he said quietly. The man raised an eyebrow.

'I'm sorry,' he said.

Saif shook his head smartly.

'No,' he said. 'They will have been picked up by another boat.'

He looked up, trying not to appear pleading. Pleading did not work, he had learned. School bullies knew that. His world was run by school bullies now.

'Can you find them for me?'

'No, but if you've actually got British qualifications, we can get you a job,' said the man from the government. 'Then you can find them yourself.'

Chapter 8

Weeks went by before Lorna got a copy of the official letter about a new doctor for the island. The council had been doing a victory dance, all delighted by the news.

> We are pleased to inform you that your application for additional GP services has been accepted. Your allocated full-time GP will be arriving on 12 April ...

It went on, but that was all she needed to hear. Her father's headaches had settled a little with some stronger medication, but she was still worried about him. She thought Sandy should have sent him to a specialist on the mainland.

A second opinion would be a wonderful thing.

This being Mure, the news was all round the village by the time she popped down to the local farm shop to pick up one of their delicious ham and piccalilli sandwiches.

'Ooh, do you think he'll be young?' old Mrs

Bruce was asking Morag, the shopkeeper. Mrs Bruce was seventy-eight, so her idea of young was anyone under the age of seventy-three.

'Don't be daft,' Morag said, filling the old lady's shopping bag for her. She didn't buy much, but she always bought the best, Mrs Bruce. 'They're all lassies now anyway, doctors. It's all girls.'

Mrs Bruce frowned. 'That's a shame,' she said, then turned to see Lorna standing there. 'Might have been a nice young man in there for you, Miss Lorna.'

'Thank you for looking out for me, Mrs Bruce,' said Lorna, smiling.

The last three men Mrs Bruce had suggested for Lorna had been: a) Iain Bruich, who was twenty years old but looked fourteen; b) Callum MacPherson, ten minutes after he'd been thrown out of his house again by his wife for his nasty night-time habits; and c) Wullie MacIver.

'That's all right, hen,' said Mrs Bruce, patting her arm in a motherly way. 'You know the right man will come along.'

Lorna and Morag, who were good friends, looked at one another. Morag had no use for men at all, but she could wrestle a good-sized calf to the ground if its ears needed syringing.

'Well, I just hope he – or she – is a good doctor,' said Lorna, a little primly, she realised.

'Actually, average will be fine,' said Morag. 'Average to not that good will still be an improvement on what we have at the moment. What? What did I say?'

Mrs Bruce pursed her lips and left the shop – she wouldn't hear a word spoken against that lovely young Dr MacAllister. Morag and Lorna burst out laughing.

Chapter 9

Saif had known that there would be a boat. His geography of Britain was hazy, but that much had been obvious. He had sat several exams, and then been given his placement. He was to be sent to an island, where he was to stay for at least two years, working.

After that, something else would happen to him, although nobody seemed clear what that would be.

But he hadn't really thought about what it would actually be like to go on a boat again.

The train had been wonderful. Surrounded by so much . . . so much normality. A rich chatter of voices, strange accents he couldn't understand. Everyone looked at him, he noticed. He knew he didn't fit in. He had very little money. His shoes were wrong, but he wasn't exactly sure how. He had found a seat by the window and relished the feeling of travelling, of moving, without waiting to be stopped, shouted at.

A woman in a uniform came through

checking tickets, and he felt a sudden moment of terror – was he going to be thrown off the train, or worse? He panicked slightly, looking for the ticket in his tattered wallet. But she glanced at the orange-striped piece of paper briefly, without interest, and moved on. Then his heart rate gradually slowed and he loosened his grip on his black bag.

For the rest of the journey, he stared out of the window, shocked at the amazing rich greenness of Great Britain; the huge open fields, some shining bright yellow; the intense weight of the grey clouds. The sky felt a lot closer here than at home, as if everything was very slightly damp. It was beautiful, he thought, but strange.

He saw no children playing in the streets of the towns they passed through. He bought an expensive sandwich from the buffet and could not finish it. He took out his English edition of *Gray's Anatomy* but grew weary. Then, with the hard-won knack of grabbing sleep whenever he needed to, he drifted off.

The boat, though. The boat was something else.

Chapter 10

A small crowd had gathered down by the quayside, and a photographer had come from the *Oban Times*.

'Seriously,' said Lorna's friend Flora, who was down there being nosy and was annoyed that everyone else was too. 'Is there really nothing else to do on Mu ... Don't answer that.'

It was a Saturday morning and they were meant to be going for coffee, but they'd seen the crowd down by the harbour wall.

There had been a lot of discussion on the matter. Not all of it pleasant. Much of it heated. And all of it ending with the sure fact that Mure needed a doctor, and no one else seemed to want to do it.

It was an odd thing to discuss on a spring day when the sun was high, the beaches were golden and filled with people, and the Atlantic wind felt soft and fresh. There were crabs and langoustine for the taking in the water. The cafés along the front were doing a roaring trade in ice cream, and the evenings were starting to get longer. It felt, on days like this, like paradise; not exactly a hardship to live somewhere so beautiful. Yet nobody, it seemed, wanted to.

He was supposed to be coming in on the early-morning ferry; except he wasn't on it, it appeared. The ship's bosun had nothing to say about it. So the crowd broke up, muttering things that were not, on the whole, kind, and Flora and Lorna had to pretend they really were just going for a coffee after all.

Chapter 11

Saif never cried. Not any more.

But if he could have, he might have then.

He had a plan, he had told himself. He had a chance now to get settled. Work. Then, as soon as he had some money, he would stop at nothing, absolutely nothing, until they were found. That was his vow. And the job paid more money than he had ever imagined he would see; more than his father had ever made, even in the good years.

But the big boat, bobbing in the choppy water ... He was on the brink of failing before he had even got started.

He could not get on. The men had shouted, telling him they were leaving, but he simply could not. Right now, at the very end of this long journey, he could not bring himself to take that step.

There was a dingy, cold coffee bar at the ferry terminal.

Saif bought a horrible milky, powdery cup of

coffee and sat down, eyed by the coffee shop owner.

This was it. The last test. He had been bought this ticket. He had nothing else; he had been given a couple of suits, and that was all – they had made sure of that. If he didn't arrive, didn't do the job he was given, then he had nothing, in a strange country. And if he disappeared and they found him, that would be the end of everything.

They had trusted him because of his professional status. They had been kind – distant, but kind. They had offered him life when his own country offered nothing but despair and death on both sides; to his utter shame.

Saif sat all day in the draughty ferry terminal, trying to make a cup of coffee last as long as he could, trying to make himself move, wander, get on his way. But there was nowhere left to go.

He glanced out. Clouds and bright bursts of sunshine crossed the sky in turn, incredibly fast. It felt like he was at the very edge of the world. There was nothing above here; nothing from here through the Faroe Islands to the North Pole. He had reached the end of the road, quite literally. He stared out at the dancing sky.

The ferry came in for its very last run of the

day. It was the evening shift, which carried workers from the mainland; post and supplies; the newspapers if they'd been missed before.

He stared at it, paralysed with fear, unable to move, feeling the breath short in his throat.

A man came in: the captain. He was wearing a uniform and a hat. Saif shrank back in his seat. Now the questions would begin. He was in the wrong place. He would be made to leave. Unwanted, again. He clutched his bag nervously, and swallowed hard.

'Hey,' said the man. He was tall and red of face, and had a beard, greying in parts. His accent was hard to understand; Saif did his best.

'Are you the refugee?'

Saif hated this word. He was a doctor, fine. A man. A Syrian, although he'd been raised in the Lebanon. But 'refugee'. That was a label of pity, of scorn, of being less than a person, of being something strange.

He nodded without saying anything.

Then the captain did a surprising thing. He sat down on the plastic chair that was nailed to the ground facing Saif.

He didn't say anything for a while. Saif looked at the freezing plastic cup of terrible coffee that he'd made last half the afternoon.

'I was shipwrecked,' said the man eventually.

'Fire in the galley. The boat sank faster than you can imagine. Blink of an eye and there was nothing solid beneath your feet at all. Nothing. We lost a good man too.'

Saif looked at him, his heart quickening.

'Took ... took me a while to get back on board,' said the captain.

He cleared his throat, gruffly.

'Anyway. I mean. If you wanted to ... '

He paused.

'The island needs a doctor,' he said quietly. 'It's not safe. That old guy, honestly. I wouldn't trust him with a wart.'

He looked Saif in the eye.

'You could ... if you wanted, you could sit up in the wheelhouse with me. Safest place to be. And you can barely see a wave. If, like, you wanted to. You know.'

Saif didn't know how to answer him. It was as if his entire voice had gone. The captain nodded quickly, then stood up to go.

'Tide's turning,' he muttered gruffly at the door.

There was silence in the large, empty terminal building. Then Saif picked up his bag.

'Wait ... please,' he managed to stutter out. The captain turned back. He didn't say anything, just nodded quietly and carried on.

Chapter 12

The curious crowd of the morning had left by the evening tide; it was getting chilly, and Mure people had their tea early. The sun was trying to shine, but the chilly wind blew down from the Arctic, whipping through the white crests of the waves in the little shingle harbour.

Lorna pulled her coat round her tightly, and worried about her dad, and all the marking of children's work that she should be doing. As she walked her little white fox terrier, Milou, along the promenade, Milou's bearded muzzle blew in the wind.

She almost ran straight into Ewan, the mainland policeman who came to Mure for the very occasional crime. Mostly it was teenagers setting barns on fire after making their own alcohol called hooch. Sometimes it was a drunk driver, although they generally only hurt themselves, by driving straight into hedges. Otherwise Ewan chatted about road safety and stranger danger at the school. The idea of stranger danger was a difficult one for the children to understand, because most people on the island had known them and their parents and grandparents for generations.

'Hey there,' said Lorna.

She and Ewan Andersson had had a very awkward couple of dates as teenagers. That was back when she used to catch the ferry to the high school in Oban and his cheery face had greeted her across the chemistry lab. But they weren't awkward with each other now. Ewan had married, presumably by chance, Laura, who had sat next to Lorna in high school – they had been seated in alphabetical order. He was a sensible, dogged man, who was not very imaginative, not a romantic. In fact, he was a perfect small-town copper, whose gentleness with difficult lads, and firmness with out-of-towners' bad parking, had made him very popular.

'What's up? Doesn't feel like a Saturday night.'

Ewan shifted uncomfortably, his radio against his hip, even though it must be useless over here.

'Yeah, I know. I've been asked to come and meet the boat.'

'Oh!' said Lorna. 'Oh yeah. I thought he wasn't coming.'

'Well, apparently he is.'

'Good,' said Lorna, meaning it. She looked out to the horizon, where, just bobbing into view, the CalMac ferry was steadily making its way towards them. She wondered what the doctor must be feeling.

'Where's he staying?'

'Oh, Mrs Laird is getting the old rectory ready.'

'You're joking.'

'Why? It's just sitting there.'

Mure hadn't managed to keep its own vicar; the last full-time one had left five years ago. Now there was a touring island vicar, who held a service every couple of weeks. He could be booked for weddings and christenings, although there weren't many christenings these days. He always looked harassed and over-worked and disapproving when he did turn up.

In contrast, Lorna's devout and beloved grandfather had often quoted that she must find 'tongues in trees, books in the running brooks, sermons in stones, and good in everything'. She had always liked this more than getting up and going to church.

'Yes, but isn't he a Muslim?'

'Can't see as that will make any difference,' said Ewan, looking at her sharply. 'I wouldn't have put you in the camp that thinks he's here to blow us all up.'

'Of course I'm not!' said Lorna, her face turning a little red. 'It just seems a bit odd, that's all.'

'I think,' said Ewan, 'he'll be pleased with a roof over his head. That's what I think, and that when you're hungry it doesn't really matter who feeds you. And it's the same when you need a doctor.'

'You Samaritan,' said Lorna, smiling, and Ewan grinned back cheerfully.

'So why are you here?' said Lorna.

Ewan frowned. 'Just . . . just to make sure.'

'What? They were expecting trouble?'

Ewan glanced around. 'I guess so, but unless they count Milou, I don't think there's going to be much.'

Sure enough, Lorna noticed a press photographer still waiting hopefully. It hardly seemed like the world's greatest scoop.

'Milou isn't trouble!'

Ewan tactfully patted the excited little dog, who immediately planted his muddy paws on the policeman's thighs, tail wagging madly.

'Why are you here?'

'Walking the dog,' said Lorna. 'Do you think I should stay and say hello? Or will that be weird and awkward?'

Ewan looked at her in a pitying way. And Lorna remembered that, though he was a dunce

37

at chemistry, and a very sloppy kisser (although they *were* only fifteen), he had uncommon good sense, which had stood him in very good stead.

'This is going to be his home,' he said gently. 'So yes. I'd likely say hello.'

Chapter 13

The boat came in slowly. One or two more people had joined them, picking up friends and relatives and parcels. Lorna tried to look welcoming and friendly and not racist. It was a harder facial expression to put on than you might think.

She saw Mrs Laird – who used to 'do' for the vicar and was obviously holding the keys to the rectory – standing nearby. She smiled at her reassuringly.

'I hope he's nice,' she said.

'I don't care if he's nice, if he can fix my varicose veins,' said Mrs Laird. She sighed. 'You know, he's not bringing a family with him.'

'Maybe he doesn't have a family.'

Mrs Laird blinked and looked at her strangely.

'Everyone has a family,' she said. 'You think he had no one to bring?'

Lorna hadn't really thought about it like that. She'd gone off to college on the mainland for four years, and had then taught in Glasgow for two years. Then she had been tempted home, or rather, had felt guilty about her dad. She was used to just getting up and going where she wanted.

Everyone came off the ferry, and drove away, and there was no sign of him. Then the crew who were finishing their shift came off. Finally, the captain came down from the wheelhouse.

Walking beside him, in a coat that looked both rather smart and also as if it totally didn't belong to him, was a tall, stooped man with a shock of black hair. His face was hidden against the wind blowing in off the harbour.

Lorna watched him slowly come ashore, and wondered what was going through his mind. What would he think of them? Would he think they were immoral Westerners who ate and drank too much? Who didn't understand the world? Would he be all right handing out birth control to the young girls? What was his English like? Would he look after her dad? Her brother Iain wasn't due back from the rigs for another couple of months, and she was getting worried about her dad again.

Ewan and Mrs Laird stepped forward, Ewan with his hand out.

'Welcome to Mure,' he said, as the photographer set off his flash, which made the man blink uncomfortably.

'Thank you,' he said, so quietly Lorna could barely hear him. His accent was gentle.

'We've got a hoose for you!' said Mrs Laird, and the man obviously didn't quite understand. So Lorna said, 'House. There's a house for you,' and he glanced up. Beneath his heavy fringe, which badly needed cutting, she glimpsed large dark eyes, incredibly weary and sad-looking, with big black shadows beneath them. He was clean-shaven, but with stubble showing through.

'Thank you.'

Lorna smiled cheerfully at him, but he looked too tired to return it.

After that, everyone stood around shuffling their feet nervously. Obviously nobody was going to ask him to the pub. The captain shook his hand and headed back to the ship for the night crossing to Harris. The sun vanished behind a cloud and rain started popping down out of nowhere.

Mrs Laird said, 'Come with me, then,' and the man picked up his suitcase. It wasn't even on wheels, Lorna noticed. How could you carry a suitcase all that way when it wasn't even on *wheels*? He held a black bag firmly in his other hand, and started to follow Mrs Laird, obediently, like a child.

He should have a little sign round his neck

that said 'Please look after this bear', thought Lorna, but she didn't say it out loud. Instead, as the little party trailed off, she said, 'I hope you'll be very happy here.' He turned back to look at her as if she'd said the stupidest thing of all time, as if anyone could possibly be happy here, and she felt awkward and slightly insulted at the same time.

And then Milou, who wasn't bothered, ran up to check out the newcomer.

At first the man flinched, and Lorna wondered: had there been dogs? Guard dogs?

But Milou kept up his cheerful licking, and finally the man relaxed a little. In a quick movement, he scratched the dog behind the ears, just for a second, before turning away again.

Saif was absolutely freezing cold. Why did people keep saying what a beautiful day it was? It wasn't a beautiful day. He was trying to force himself to think in English now. He was trying to stop translating the words in his head, but simply to think in the language all the time.

He couldn't understand the tiny woman who had broken veins crackling in her cheeks. She walked around the dark, chilly house, pointing things out to him that didn't make any sense.

There was a boiler, with various buttons to

be pressed. Everything – the heavy curtains, the old bedspread – felt slightly damp to the touch. He put his bag down and looked around. Mrs Laird – 'rrrrd' he repeated to himself, 'LaiRRRRD' – showed him how to work the kettle, as if such a thing would be a strange foreign object to him. But she didn't show him the mixer tap, which was strange to him.

As she backed awkwardly out of the door, she wished him well, and told him she could come in twice a week to clean if he'd like.

When she'd gone, he went around turning on as many lamps as he could find. But this still didn't do much to lift the gloom. Then he pulled open the curtains – it was still light outside, even at eight o'clock. He hadn't realised that it stayed light so late so far north. A neatly trimmed lawn went to the end of a small slope, then dropped off a cliff. Beyond was a vast sea, with the mountains of the mainland just visible. The sky too was vast, freshly washed by the rainfall.

It looked like the furthest edge of the world.

Anyway. What he needed, first of all, was a mobile signal, which he didn't seem to have. And some internet, which he didn't seem to have either. The one thing he'd managed to hold together, more or less, was to keep his mobile number. He'd been given a new British number, but he had to keep his old number. He had to.

Of all the benefits of being here, in this safe, cold, comfortable land, he didn't have the only thing he really needed. A way to be found, when he felt so very lost.

Chapter 14

'You do NOT look well,' said Lorna crossly to her dad. She had popped in to see him on the way to school. Ever since her mum had died from breast cancer eight years before, her father had completely given up. She could understand. She really could. She could see that without her mum around nagging him to eat his greens and lay off the whisky, he couldn't be expected to do everything himself. And of course he missed her. They all did, but the hole in her dad's life was absolutely huge.

There had been plenty of nice ladies, many widowed or divorced, who made him lasagnes and looked like they would be perfectly happy to become the second Mrs MacLeod. He was in good shape, after all, after a life of hard labouring, and had kept his own hair, which made him quite a catch on their small island.

But he wasn't interested, not at all. He refused to give up work, and the rest of the time, day or night, Lorna would find him staring at the television without looking at it. He showed no interest in anything apart from, occasionally, after a few whiskies, looking at his wedding album.

She had been patient, understanding, kind, as good a daughter as she could possibly manage.

It was driving her crazy.

'Did you just sleep in this chair?'

'Don't fuss me,' said Angus.

'I'm not fussing you. I'm asking a question. Why did you sleep in your chair?'

'Just fell asleep. My head was sore.'

Lorna looked at him. His grey stubble was showing. He looked uncared for. His eyes weren't clearly focused, although he hadn't been drinking. (She checked the level of the whisky bottle. It made her feel bad to do that, but she did it anyway.)

'How sore? Worse or better than usual?'

Angus grunted. Lorna frowned.

'Come on,' she said, sighing. This was yet another thing that was going to get her into trouble with the Parent Teacher Association. 'Let's go and get you checked out.'

There was a fuss at the surgery. Jeannie was looking stressed.

It was Mrs Green from up the close, a well-known

46

busybody who upset many people with her sharp comments. It wasn't nice to come out and have your parking/hairstyle/childcare methods attacked. In her kinder moments Lorna thought Mrs Green was lonely, and that every community had a Mrs Green. In her less kind moments Lorna remembered that Mrs Green had a husband, a tidy little council house and a perfectly nice life, and some people were just born like that.

'I don't want to see the new doctor,' Mrs Green was saying loudly. 'I'm not prejudiced. I don't have a racist bone in my body. I'm just saying, life's cheap where he comes from, isn't it? That's a fact. If he's watched kiddies die, he's not going to be very interested in my ... Well, that's private. And does he speak English?'

'Of course he speaks English,' sighed Jeannie, sounding as if she'd said that a few times already that morning, which she had. 'Now you can wait and see Dr MacAllister, but I'm warning you, it might be a long wait.'

Mrs Green sniffed. 'Yes. We're not stupid.'

Jeannie's face remained impressively blank. Her eyes flickered to Lorna with a slight hint of panic. Everyone looked anxious.

'Um, whatever you have,' said Lorna.

'Great,' said Jeannie loudly and sternly. 'Well, *you* can have an appointment straight away.'

'How's it going?' hissed Lorna.

'Everyone wants to have a look,' said Jeannie. 'Nobody wants to be first.'

'Oh, for goodness' sake. He's a foreigner, not a beast from the moon. We'll look unwelcoming.'

'Everyone's perfectly welcoming. Until it's time to show him their privates.'

'I wouldn't be a GP for all the tea in China,' said Lorna, not for the first time.

'No, neither will any other bugger. That's our problem,' said Jeannie, with unusual force.

Despite her scorn for the other patients, Lorna was a little nervous as she opened the door. The room had been put together quickly when the news that the new doctor was coming had finally sunk in. It used to belong to old Dr MacAllister, before he got too old to work. It was therefore full of ancient medical equipment: a plaster skull with a map of the human brain; some scary bulbs and thick tubes that were more suited to a vet's.

It was spotlessly clean, though, and when she entered, nervously, Dr Hassan had his back to her, soaping his arms. He was wearing a smart striped shirt; it was a little too large for him. His shoulders were broad, slightly stooped. He was very thin, particularly for Mure, where people tended towards comfortable farming stock, and he needed a haircut.

She cleared her throat politely, as Angus sat down on the grey plastic seat. The doctor turned around.

Chapter 15

Saif tried his best to keep calm.

He didn't recognise the woman straight away, but he smiled vaguely. Here he was. First patient. The exams he'd had to resit rushed through his head; the English words for everything that might come up. Please let him diagnose properly. Please let him be able to communicate. The way they spoke here wasn't like any English he'd ever heard.

'Please,' he said. 'Sit.'

Then he realised that of course the older man in the room was already sitting, and this must be his daughter.

'Hello.'

'Hello,' said the woman, smiling uneasily. She looked awkward and embarrassed. Well, this was not a great start, thought Saif, scratching the back of his head. He felt tongue-tied.

'What seems to be the problem?'

If it hadn't been such a long time since she'd dated, Lorna certainly wouldn't have reacted as she did. She thought of herself as quite a level-headed person on the whole. Normally.

But it had been a while.

Really quite a long while.

And this wasn't remotely normal.

Bloody hell.

She hadn't noticed when she'd seen the stooped figure the day before just how handsome he was. Now he turned round, and she froze.

Don't be silly, she told herself. You are an idiot who is buried away on this island with just sheep and your dad and small children for company, and you have officially gone mad. You need to take Flora's advice and go get drunk in Glasgow for the weekend and see if you can pull.

She risked another glance.

Bugger! Now she was blushing. Right. She wouldn't look at him. This was awful. She was behaving like a fourteen-year-old. It had never crossed her mind that he might be . . . She bit the inside of her mouth quite hard.

'My father's having head . . . head things. Headaches,' she added, like a bumbling fool, barely able to get the words out.

Head things? thought Saif. Did she think he was an idiot? Possibly unqualified? That he didn't speak English?

51

'Head things?' he repeated, staring at her to make sure she knew he understood.

'Headaches,' she repeated, looking very embarrassed.

Saif noticed her blushing and felt embarrassed himself. It was as if he was some animal in a zoo, and she hadn't expected him to talk.

'I'm right here,' said the man from his seat. 'And I'm fine.'

'No you're not, Dad,' said the woman, dropping to his level and not looking at Saif. 'Tell the doctor.'

Saif sat down and tried to adopt the open bedside manner the leaflets had said were normal in the UK. His hands felt sweaty.

'Well. I just get a headache now and again.'

'Any particular time of day?' said Saif.

'Um, mornings mostly.'

Saif nodded.

'Any tiredness? Vomiting?'

'Yes. Yes. I'm tired.'

'That's because you're still working a bit. On the farm,' the woman said, explaining it to Saif.

'Well, I wasn't tired before,' said Angus.

'Well, you weren't in your seventies before!' she said. Saif frowned a little, because this was exactly how his sister used to talk to his own father.

The woman saw it and flushed again. There was a pause.

'Any dizziness?' said Saif, writing notes on his pad. He could write for now; learning how to use the system on the computer would have to wait.

'Yes, now you mention it.'

Saif's heart sank. Why couldn't his first patient have one of the common complaints seen by doctors – sleeplessness, anxiety, piles and viruses? Why did he have to see something that was perhaps serious straight away? Would they accuse him of being a worrier if he sent everyone off to hospital?

Or not up to the job, if he didn't?

He realised, at least, that he didn't have at the back of his mind the question of whether paying for treatment would be too much for the family. This was new to him, and remarkable.

Also, he'd need to phone the consultant at the nearest hospital. He didn't like talking on the phone yet; he wasn't quite confident about his fluency. Face to face was fine, but nuance was lost on the telephone line. Perhaps Jeannie could help. She'd been incredibly kind.

He checked Angus's vital signs and blood pressure. None of it was at all encouraging.

'I'm going to send you to the hospital,' he said. 'Let them take a look at you.'

'Are you sure?' said the woman, looking panicked.

Saif frowned. Were people going to doubt everything he said because he was foreign?

'Yes, I am sure,' he said bluntly. 'I would like them to look at your father.'

The daughter nodded. 'Okay. Will you get us an appointment? Send us a letter about it?'

Saif shook his head.

'I will call them,' he said. 'I want you to go there now. Straight away.'

His voice was strong and clear. There would be no argument.

Chapter 16

The doctor's voice had sounded to Lorna like a cold hand clutching at her heart. She waited while Jeannie sorted the paperwork. The receptionist gave her a caring look.

'I'm sure it's nothing. New doctors are always over-cautious. I saw it all the time on the mainland. Seriously, you'll be home this afternoon. I wouldn't even call Iain.'

'Hmm,' said Lorna. 'I hope you're right.' There couldn't be anything wrong with Dad. There couldn't. Not after what they'd been through with her mother. She dreaded that mainland hospital again with its awful sterile smell, its endless waiting under buzzing fluorescent lights.

'I'm sure I am.'

There was a pause.

'So, apart from the fact that he was a bit nervous, what did you think of our new doctor?'

Lorna didn't say anything for a second.

'I know!' said Jeannie.

'What? What do you know?'

'Super-hot, right?'

'I just . . . he just wasn't what I expected.'

'You weren't expecting a gorgeous hunk?'

'No wedding ring,' said Lorna.

Jeannie gave her a sharp look. 'Mmm.'

'What . . . I mean, does he talk about where he's been?'

'I've only spoken to him for an hour, and most of that was about prescribing pads.'

'Oh,' said Lorna.

'And he keeps going off to use the computer and making a fuss about the Wi-Fi.'

'Oh. So you don't know anything about him?'

'I don't think it's our place to ask,' said Jeannie, kindly. 'Do you?'

Lorna shook her head as something buzzed out of the printer.

'Here's your letter to take to the hospital,' said Jeannie. She paused. 'Good luck,' she added.

Chapter 17

It was three weeks before Lorna saw Saif again.

Three awful, dreadful weeks of horrible misery, as they went from one place to another. It went from that ghastly heart-stopping moment on that first day, to test following test. Then they sat in a grim hospital room with a kindly older woman who gazed at the charts on her desk and the computer in front of her and almost anywhere else before she spoke. She told them, in a voice so quiet Lorna could hardly hear it and Angus couldn't hear it at all, that yes, there was a small brain tumour there. It could probably be treated with radiotherapy, but they'd need to check to make sure.

The two of them had sat, completely stunned. They had been unable to do anything except somehow thank the doctor and apologise for taking up her time. It had been as if they were cluttering up her office with their pathetic complaints.

It wasn't until they got into the car, ready

57

for the long drive back to the last ferry of the evening, that they began to take it in. Angus sat in the front and gave a long sigh.

'Guess that's it, then.'

Lorna looked at him.

'Of course it isn't! She says it can be treated!'

'She gave us a leaflet,' said Angus. 'That always means bad news. They don't print up leaflets for good news.'

'I'm sure that's not true,' scolded Lorna.

'I'm just glad your mum's not here to see it,' said Angus, and Lorna shot him a look.

'Don't you start that,' she said. 'You start that and you might as well just go drown yourself in a vat of whisky right now. And where does that get us? Or to be more precise, me?'

Angus sniffed.

'I don't fancy coming back here every two days for six weeks.'

'Well, you're a long time dead,' said Lorna. She was cross with herself for being angry with him. It wasn't his fault. Brain tumours, the doctor had muttered, weren't anybody's fault. They just happened. And this one could definitely be treated. They would do everything they could.

Thank goodness for the Easter holidays. Easter was late that year, which meant that school was out just at the same time as the full bloom of the daffodils. Bluebells were yet to come. Children wrapped in jumpers and scarves and wellingtons were running across the vast golden beaches under the wide sky, with its rushing clouds as white as the dancing tips of the cold waves.

But for Lorna, it meant nothing but worry. She lay in bed at night thinking about losing her only parent. She tried to put on a happy face when she saw him. She sat through long hours in stupid waiting rooms, trying to chat when there was nothing to say. There was simply the terror lying behind the small talk, behind the blaring television on the wall above their heads. The television that couldn't be switched off or turned down, even when they were the only people in the waiting room.

There were missed travel connections and hotel rooms they couldn't really afford. Once or twice they took other people's appointments, and on and on.

As usual, the whole of Mure came together to help them. Dishes appeared on their steps every day. Laundry just disappeared and turned up again. (Angus hadn't locked his front door in his life.)

Mrs Collins at the school took on the bulk of Lorna's paperwork. The farm boys came up and hung around, desperately looking for something to do to help Angus, their old boss.

But no one could help Lorna where it truly mattered: inside.

After three weeks, she cracked. This couldn't go on. She was in tears half the time. Her brother Iain couldn't get back from the rigs for another two months. She couldn't keep on doing this alone, not if she was going to return to school.

She went back to the doctor, by herself.

She had thought about Saif quite a lot. She tried to tell herself that she was just wondering how he was getting on. But every time some of the endless paperwork came from the hospital, she would see his name. She liked seeing his name.

But that was only brief seconds here and there. She'd been too busy on the whole, too worried to think about anything. She hadn't had a chance to grab a coffee or a glass of wine with Jeannie to hear the gossip. Even if they all needed a catch-up, a big one.

She'd moved back into the farmhouse. Of course she had. What else could she do? Every evening, she'd help Dad up to bed. (He shouldn't be taking whisky with his painkillers, but as he pointed out, he was over seventy, which had to count for something, didn't it?) Then she couldn't sleep. The old house creaked because of the wooden slats in the thick stone walls. The animals outside in the pens shifted and bellowed. Angus of course woke at 5 a.m. – the habit of a lifetime. She woke then too, but she was lucky to get to sleep before two or three, and sometimes not at all.

She looked, she knew, completely awful. Her hair needed a trim. Normally she would find time to get it done in Oban. This was no disrespect to Phyllis Weir, the local hairdresser. Phyllis travelled about doing the old ladies' shampoos and sets, and was great for a gossip and a cup of tea. But she didn't understand if you asked her for anything honeyed or naturalesque, or if you mentioned Jennifer Aniston.

Lorna had huge bags under her eyes and could do almost nothing without bursting into tears. Despite Mrs Collins' help, the paperwork for the new term was still a lot of work. It was the summer term too, which meant it was full of school trips and outings and shows. She hadn't touched a single bit of the paperwork, none of it. When she tried to look at it, the words swam in front of her eyes.

She remembered she had to pick up special cream for her father where he'd been burned by the radiotherapy, and that they'd run out of milk. She needed to have a big meeting with Angus's farm manager. There were bills piling up in the letter box.

She couldn't cope, however much help she had. She just couldn't. She was completely crushed. And if that has ever happened to you, you'll know how difficult it is to do more than just the tiniest basics.

Chapter 18

'Next?' said Saif dully, glancing briefly at the computer. He could work the system now and could read notes and book appointments online. He was a prescription pad in motion. People had tried to be cheery and welcoming – well, most of them – but he had absolutely no interest in them at all. He only wanted to have a daily look through the lists of the charities: Médecins Sans Frontières, the Red Crescent, Save the Children. Anywhere that posted lists; anywhere at all. He was just waiting and waiting.

As for the town, people were friendly but didn't intrude. That was the islanders' way. It wasn't exactly as if all talk stopped whenever he walked into a shop or the post office ... well, sometimes it did. But social life here seemed to revolve around the pub or the church, neither of which applied to him really. And his thoughts weren't with the people he looked after. Although he treated them as thoroughly and carefully as he could. They could sense, too, that he didn't feel he belonged;

that he didn't truly want to. It was not a problem he thought he could solve: loneliness.

He had started taking long walks. At first, being cold had made him miserable. Reminding him of so many long days and nights, sleeping whenever he could. Now, when it was clear, he liked the fresh pink mornings, the vast sky. The stars were further away here. But you could still see them; not like in the cities, where there was too much light.

And the beaches; he had never seen such beaches. They went on, cool, pale pink and white sand, for miles and miles, empty. Nobody there. A spot at the end of the world with nobody there. Why? he found himself thinking. Why wasn't everyone here? Why couldn't they bring them all home to this safe, quiet, stable place? Not just the useful ones, like him?

But he couldn't complain. As soon as they found out he was actually a normal doctor, and that he wanted to be left alone, they'd done just that. And they were pleased that he would happily prescribe antibiotics. With his other worries, Saif was a little bit beyond worrying about the morality of prescribing too many antibiotics. He couldn't cook, though. That was a problem. He knew Mrs Laird would happily have cooked for him every day. But he found her shepherd's pie and stews very tasteless, and he wasn't sure that she always remembered he didn't eat pork. But he had to eat something.

He blinked, woken from his thoughts.

'Um, hello?'

He didn't recognise the young woman sitting in front of him.

'Hello again,' she said, and he smiled slightly shyly. Obviously he knew he stood out, but also, everyone on the island knew everyone else on the island, so someone knowing who he was didn't really count. It had been like that in Damascus once; the feeling was familiar somehow. It was nice, he supposed. To feel you belonged.

'How can I help?'

'Um,' she said. He glanced at the computer. Lorna. Lorna MacLeod. One of the easier names to say. He'd already had big problems with Eilidh, Euan, Teurlach and Mhairi.

'Well. I've been having trouble sleeping.'

Saif looked at her. He hadn't slept more than three hours per night for over half a year. His phone was always blinking at him, always glowing, even when he couldn't get a signal.

'Uh huh,' he said.

'I'm under a lot of pressure with my father.'

It sounded like 'faither', the way she said it. He was beginning to understand the rhythms of the sing-songy local voice. He noticed how its words ran on and had an unusual lilt. But the first time he heard Gaelic spoken in the waiting room, he'd had to take a step back before he realised it was a different language and not his English failing him. He didn't know it, but he'd started to take on some of the lilt himself.

'Yes,' he said.

'And my job and the farm and ... I'm feeling a bit overwhelmed.'

They looked at each other. Lorna was hopeful that he would take it from here in his role as doctor. Saif was puzzled as to what on earth she wanted.

'Um, yes?' he said.

'So I wondered if you could help.'

'I'm a doctor.'

'I know, but I wondered if you could maybe ... help me sleep or something.'

'But I help you if there is something wrong with you.'

Lorna felt tears pricking her eyelids.

'Well, obviously, there is something wrong with me.'

Saif remembered her now. He leaned forward.

'I understand. Your father is sick, yes?'

Lorna nodded. 'He's in treatment. And I have to do everything. And I feel like I can't cope.'

Saif blinked. Lorna couldn't help looking at his long eyelashes. Then she felt guilty for staring, but he hadn't noticed.

'Well,' he said, looking up. 'You have to cope.'

'Sorry?' said Lorna, confused.

'You have a difficult thing to do.'

'Yes.'

'Many people have difficult things to do.'

There was a pause as Lorna tried to work out what he was saying.

'You mean . . . you won't give me anything to help me sleep?'

'What time do you go to bed?'

'Eleven? Normal time. But I just lie there thinking. It just goes round and round in my head.'

'Go to bed at nine,' said Saif. Lorna stared at him, horrified.

'That's your advice? But if I can't sleep at eleven, how will I possibly be able to sleep at nine?'

Saif shrugged.

'A good routine. Perhaps some more exercise?'

Lorna went bright pink.

'I'm IN THE CAR ALL DAY DRIVING MY FATHER TO THE HOSPITAL,' she shouted.

Outside, the waiting room fell silent.

'No,' said Saif. 'I am sorry. It would be wrong. Pills are not right for you.'

There was another pause. Lorna felt so angry that her heart pounded in her chest. She wanted very badly to shout at him again.

He leant forward.

'You are unhappy,' he said, in what was meant to be a friendly tone, but came out clipped as he searched for precisely the right words to say. 'Because sad things are happening in your life. How do drugs help with that? You are sad. Feel the sadness. If you came in here and said "everything in my life is perfect and wonderful, yet every day is terrible" – well then, yes, we have a problem. But you are worried because of your father. That is right for you to be. You are sad because there is work to be done to help him. That is right for you to be also. Then, when he is better, your sadness will pass. This is normal life, you understand?'

'I. Just. Need. Something. To. Help. Me. Sleep.'

He shook his head.

'No. Listen to me on this. You are normal. If you take pills to help you sleep, then you will always need pills to help you sleep, even though it is normal. Even though it is right to feel as you feel. Sad is not an illness.'

Lorna blinked.

'How do you know?'

There was a long pause.

'I will tell you. I know.'

'So you won't give me anything?' She looked like she was going to cry.

Saif tapped a few more buttons on his computer and looked at her father's results from the hospital.

'Yes,' he said. 'I can see what is happening with your father, and how he is responding to treatment.'

He looked straight at her.

'I do not think you should give up hope. I have hope to give you.'

She stood up, utterly enraged. He wanted to say sorry, but he didn't know how.

'Thank you,' she said stiffly, which Saif had learned, quite correctly, was what British people said when they wanted to get away from you.

He nodded, and watched her as she left.

Chapter 19

It took several more weeks – and several nights spent lying awake cursing Saif's name – before Lorna's insomnia finally started to lift. During those weeks she nearly fell asleep while driving and cried at everything. She cried over a roadkill rabbit and a dead seagull, even though she felt about seagulls the way most people who don't live on islands feel about rats. She was clumsy, behind in her paperwork and felt sick and hopeless half the time. If only that useless doctor could have helped her!

Eventually, as the nights continued to grow shorter and shorter, she started to sleep again. As the wind coming in from the North Atlantic turned breezy and welcome, rather than cold and cutting, she finally found that going to bed as early as she could helped. In fact, she went to bed as soon as she'd given her father his last dose of medication (which she had thought about stealing, but then, with a sigh, had decided not to).

It was annoying to think that the stupid doctor had been right – and she was annoyed at herself. She'd gone in to see him, aiming to be so friendly, and he had been blunt and disapproving, just like a real doctor. It had been a difficult thing to ask for, and a very solid refusal.

But somehow she hadn't defied him, or nipped in to Dr MacAllister (a famously soft touch) for a second opinion. She'd stuck to it.

And it was true about her dad. The tumour did appear to be shrinking. It was horrible and the treatment seemed to be taking for ever, but it was doing something.

She was going to bed nice and early. Yes, all right, so *that* part had been helpful. That was very annoying. But it meant that when she got into bed she knew that she had three full hours to fall asleep. The light still beamed through the curtains. And that had a lulling effect on her, gradually calming the urge to toss and turn on the pillows. But it also meant, she thought crossly, that she had not a second to herself all evening. She had to sort out dinner, since if it were up to her father, he'd just fry up anything and serve it with beans.

Of course she woke up incredibly early, but oddly she didn't mind that so much. She used the time to walk Milou – and Lowith, one of her father's old working dogs. As a farming man he was not keen on keeping pets, but he never got rid of a dog that was too old to work. Instead he let them slink around the barn and sleep beside the old Aga in the kitchen if it was chilly at night. Lorna would accuse him of being a softie, and he'd grunt crossly and pet the old dog gently with his hand.

A bit more exercise was helping to clear her head and tire her out a bit. It was another thing that that stupid doctor had been right about.

This morning, she crammed a beret onto her unruly curls – it wasn't yet that warm early in the morning. She pulled on a huge old jacket – so old that nobody could remember who it had first belonged to. Then she headed into the fresh morning, feeling like the only person awake in the world.

It was wonderfully clear and bright out there. The sun was showing the promise of warmth. It lit the sky from end to end in a pale blue that blended into the wide white of the huge, seemingly endless beach below the farm. Small mounds of seaweed waved a little, but most of the beach was completely flawless, as if it had been designed for a film set. She could see another dog miles away, hopping about its owner. Apart from that they were completely alone at this time in the morning, even in a place where people rose early.

'Milou! Lowith!' she called, as she did every morning, in a fruitless attempt to stop them running into the surf. There they splashed as happily as their creaky old bones would let them. Then they staggered back guiltily, dripping water everywhere, even as she told them they wouldn't be allowed in the kitchen any more.

She breathed in the clear morning air. It felt sweet and fresh on her tongue. She shouted for the dogs, who of course ignored her. So she left them to it and simply strolled briskly, feeling the cool breeze on her face. She was delighted, as she always was, by the bright turquoise of the water. It was as clean, she thought, as any you'd find anywhere in the world.

She walked quite a way. She was charmed by the waves and by the clear shifting shades of green. She had an odd feeling that she didn't recognise at first. Then gradually she realised that the salty spray felt good and fresh on her skin. And eventually she became aware that what she was feeling was a sense of well-being, of calm.

She was feeling calm. She was sleeping again. She was gradually pulling it back together. Well, there was a long way to go. But she was definitely feeling better.

It was still pretty cold, but the sun was warming her a little and she risked slipping off her shoes and socks. The pale sand felt good beneath her toes. She walked towards the waves. The dogs suddenly turned to prance towards her, expecting her to join in and play with them.

She jumped over the white surf at the edge of the pure sand, straight in, ankle deep. Then she yelled out loud. It was completely freezing, like plunging your feet into a bowl of ice.

'Argh!' she yelled as the dogs wagged their tails. 'You lied to me! You told me this was going to be good!'

She chased and splashed them in the clear water, and laughed as they frolicked around her. Her feet were turning blue, but the sun felt warmer on her neck and shoulders as she ran up and down the surf.

She hardly noticed another dog come to join them. Then she recognised the normally calm bundle of fur as Mrs Laird's spoiled Scottie dog, and she turned round to say hello.

He was far closer than she'd expected. In fact, he was standing right there, and she was incredibly embarrassed that he'd seen her jumping up and down, almost dancing, thinking she was alone.

'Oh my God,' she said. 'Um. Dr Hassan. Hello.'

He barely turned to look at her, and she felt instantly worse. His large brown eyes were fixed on the horizon.

'Hello,' he said. 'Sorry. I was walking Mrs Laird's dog.'

But he wasn't, she thought. He'd been standing still, staring out to sea.

'Waiting for someone?' she asked, as a joke, then immediately wished she hadn't.

'Yes,' said Saif. He looked embarrassed, as if he'd said something he shouldn't have.

There was another one of those awkward pauses.

'So how are you?' he asked. 'You seem better.'

Lorna bit her lip. She was annoyed with him for noticing.

'Hmm,' she said. 'Well.'

'You know, if you take sleeping pills, it makes you very ... what is the word? Groggy. It makes you very groggy in the morning.'

'You're not at work,' said Lorna suddenly, half smiling at him. He looked so serious standing there. 'Come on,' she said. 'It's a beautiful day. Come in the water.'

He blinked at her in the sunshine.

'You are serious?'

'It's lovely!'

She tried kicking a few drops in his direction.

He leapt back, and she was worried she'd upset him in some odd way.

Then the most surprising thing happened. He laughed.

'That is . . . that is FREEZING!' he said.

'Maybe you're too soft,' she said, and he smiled again. She'd never seen him smile; she hadn't thought he could.

The next thing she knew, he'd kicked off the boots he was wearing and had run straight into the chilly surf.

Saif hardly knew what he was doing. It was her laughing face. It was finding out that someone had actually taken his advice and it had worked. It was the fresh new early-summer warmth in the air. It was the sense, suddenly, of the world renewing.

It hadn't been the same where he'd grown up. There were heavy-flowering plants in the late summer. Many, like bougainvillea, filled courtyards with colour. And there were oranges and lemons, of course. But not this gradual greening of the land, this softening of the island from something barren and wild and strange. Every day the shades became deeper and gentler. At first he'd barely been aware of the new leaves, the grass beginning to kick over his shoes. Now, the world had woken up without him noticing.

Part of him hated the changing of the seasons, which was so marked here. The light was astonishing. He felt further away with every longer evening. Time was pushing him ahead in a rush, carrying him away from everything he knew. But he couldn't regret that on a morning like today, with a smiling girl splashing in the water. He didn't want to be so gloomy all the time. He had loved growing up in multi-cultural, relaxed Beirut, with all its dangers. He had adored his time at medical school. He had married for love, and had headed back to settle in sleepy, devout Damascus, land of his forefathers. And then . . .

Oh, how he missed the man he had once been.

Now he found himself leaping about in freezing cold water, thousands of miles from home, grinning and trying to avoid three panting dogs. He splashed at Lorna, happy to see her outdoors and looking a million times better than she had in his surgery. She splashed back, barely feeling the cold as the sun on her back rose high in the sky and promised the most beautiful of days. She managed to drench him and he yelled back, laughing, and they came to a halt.

Lorna found she was out of breath.

'Sorry about that,' she said. 'I couldn't resist.'

'You are not in the least bit sorry,' he said, his lips twitching. 'Is this a tradition of these islands?'

'Consider yourself baptised,' said Lorna, then paused, stepping out of the surf. 'Um, sorry.'

Saif shook his head.

'Do not worry, Miss MacLeod,' he said. 'I am from Damascus. We're practically heathens as it is.'

He shook some of the water from his hair.

'You definitely seem better,' he said, glancing at her. Her cheeks were flushed pink.

'So do you,' she replied cheekily, and watched as he blinked.

'I discharge you from being my patient,' he said.

'Thanks,' said Lorna. 'And call me Lorna.'

'Saif,' said Saif gravely, and she grinned.

Then, suddenly, his eyes caught the horizon again, and it was like shutters coming down. And now she understood. He was not walking. He was waiting.

They headed slowly back up the soft white sand, not quite together.

'Your family . . . ' she started, but he cut her

off with a quick shake of his head. There was a pause.

'Well, I'd better go,' she said. 'Get Dad's breakfast.'

'It was nice to see you,' he said. 'Although obviously now I am going to go down with pleurisy.'

'You can fix it by not doing anything and going to bed at nine p.m.,' said Lorna cheekily.

'Hmm,' he said, his mouth lifting a little. They headed off in separate directions, as the dogs took a little longer to say goodbye.

Chapter 20

After that, it was surprising how many mornings they would meet, and paddle, sometimes. But only when the weather was clear. Lorna didn't care about the weather, but Saif still disliked constant rain and tended to stay away. They would talk a little, of this and that. Lorna spoke a lot about Mure, and what it was like. And she taught him a little Gaelic, which greatly surprised his patients.

Saif did not talk quite so much. Or rather, he realised how much he had missed simple friendship, and he was a good listener. He was interested in what she had to say, and would respond. But he said nothing about how he had arrived here, or what it had been like. He would talk a little about Damascus, its pretty squares and late-night eating – he found it odd that the little restaurant by the harbour stopped serving at 8 p.m. He was used to eating dinner at eleven. He liked, too, to talk about his carefree student days in Beirut.

But he mentioned nobody: not his parents, not brothers or sisters, not a wife. He wore no ring, but Lorna knew that didn't mean anything.

It was one hour, right at the beginning of their busy days. It was the only moment when, for doctor and teacher, there weren't a million claims on their time and attention. A time when there were no demanding, cranky parents; overworked colleagues; patients who were horribly sick or worried. It was simple time to themselves, out of the rush of everything that was going on in their lives. Just the clear sky, the herons dipping their long necks in the water. One morning a group of fat seals came up to sunbathe by the edge of the harbour.

It felt to Lorna like a breathing space; a break; a small piece of grace. That was all it was, she told herself sternly. Even on the mornings when she wasn't quite sure she believed it herself.

Chapter 21

'Of course you're completely bonkers,' said her best friend Flora. They were sitting in the snug bar of the Harbour Rest, an ancient wooden pub next to the fishing boats. The place still smelled of brine and pipe tobacco a decade after the smoking ban.

'I'm not bonkers,' said Lorna. 'I'm just being friendly.'

Her chum gave her a long, deep look. Not much got past Flora, who'd lived in London for seven years before coming home, and saw herself as pretty street-smart.

'Friendly like a FOX,' she said.

'It's not like that,' said Lorna.

And it wasn't. Was it? They talked about little things. Or rather she talked mostly and he seemed happy to listen.

'So he just looks lovely and keeps his mouth shut, and he's like totally a doctor and everything?' said Flora. 'I hope you realise he sounds completely made up.'

'I'm not sure he understands half of what I'm saying,' said Lorna 'But I just need someone to say it to. Do you know what I mean?'

'You can say it to me,' said Flora, who had problems of her own.

'Well, I can't, can I,' said Lorna. 'The moment I set foot in your farmhouse I'm either run over, yelled at or set to work.'

'It is a little busy,' said Flora.

There was a pause while they sipped what the Harbour Rest called a cappuccino. Lorna waited for Flora to say how much better the coffee was in London, which Flora duly did, and then they could move on.

'So do you ... do you *fancy* him?'

'I'm not twelve!' said Lorna crossly.

'So that means yes.'

'It does not!'

'It so does!'

Lorna shook her head forcefully.

'Well, it doesn't matter anyway. He doesn't ... he doesn't talk about his family at all. He might have a wife out there.'

'He might not.'

'Children ... who knows?'

'You could ask.'

'I don't want to.'

'Because you fancy him so much.'

'I don't want to talk about it.'

'Ooooh!'

Chapter 22

He knew he could ask Lorna. She might know people, or be able to find something ... or it might help just to tell her. She was so kind, so caring. But selfishly, he treasured what he'd been doing for days. He valued the hell he waded through every day, with no success. The Red Crescent had nothing. Doctors Without Borders had nothing. Not a word. It was as if they had never been there. As if their existence had been blanked out. And he refused to believe it.

He spoke endlessly to voluntary groups; to consulates; to any friends who were still there with any kind of phone access at all, although there were fewer and fewer of them. Barely anyone who could find a way out was still there. He knew that if anything could be done, if anyone could be found, the news would appear on his phone first, if it was to appear at all.

And even if, by some miracle, they reached Scotland without telling him, without anyone knowing that they had found him, they would catch the ferry from Oban like everyone else. It would arrive on time just as it did every single day. How else would you cross such a dangerous body of water? You couldn't.

He knew that Jeannie and the others in the village thought him odd, rude. Though he just thought he was being organised. He didn't hang around and chit-chat. That was for sure. He also didn't like the instant coffee Jeannie made for him, though she meant it kindly.

He was being selfish, not telling Lorna about his past, his life. These early mornings were the only time he felt like a normal person all day.

Chapter 23

'You're coming!'

Saif was only half listening, but he turned away when he heard that. There was a minor heatwave. It had taken everyone by surprise, but it was perfect because they had the soft white sand warm beneath their bare feet. The tourists hadn't had the chance to scramble to the beaches yet, or even get away. It felt like a gift, the sun giving warmth before the official start of summer.

The dogs didn't like it at all. They stayed in the water or panted in the shade. They came from generations of dogs who could sleep in a snowstorm, hardy and stalwart.

'What?' he said.

Lorna was wearing a Breton top and cropped jeans. It was Saturday morning. She'd worked long and hard at her marking the previous evening in the hope that she could have a weekend off, whatever that might look like. Her father was sleepy, coming to the end of his treatment. Lorna was hoping this was a sign that he was getting better. Whenever the animals on the farm got sick, sleep was the best thing for them.

So she was carefree this morning, feeling the joy of an empty day ahead without marking or hospital appointments or too many chores. And tonight was the village ceilidh, the Gaelic dance which happened once a month and which everyone had to go to. There wasn't really any option. Ollie the vet would dance with old Mrs Kelpie from the sweetshop. Ewan the policeman would make sure everyone got home, more or less, afterwards. And the band were incredible.

'Coming to what?'

'It's the May dance!' Lorna said. But his face remained blank. 'Dancing. You can dance, can't you?'

Saif frowned.

'No.'

'Well, everyone has to go. It supports the hotel out of season, and the band and the community and, well, basically everything.'

'This sounds quite a lot like moral blackmail.'

'Yup,' said Lorna cheerfully, throwing Milou a stick, which he brought back gracefully.

'Do I have to wear a skirt thing?'

'SAIF! You've been here for AGES! You LIVE HERE! Deal with it, you big racist! It's not a skirt.'

Saif smiled at that.

'Aye, all right.'

'Did you just say "aye"?'

'No.'

'You did! You said "aye" when you meant "yes".'

'I'm sure I didn't.'

'I think you did!'

There was a pause.

'You *could* try—'

'I don't want any haggis.'

'I'm just saying I think you should try it.'

'No.'

They walked on, both enjoying the feel of the sun on their backs.

'You're coming.'

'I'm not wearing a sk— kilt thing.'

'Kilt. It's called a kilt. Not a kilt thing.'

'Well.'

'You don't have to. Just wear something comfortable for dancing. Do you have anything comfortable? You dress like Niles from *Frasier*.'

'I don't know who that is.'

'That's probably just as well. Look. It doesn't matter what you wear.' She glanced at him. 'You should come, you know. You don't want people thinking you're weird.'

Saif blinked.

'As long as I'm looking after them, what do I care what people think?'

'*All* the people?' said Lorna.

Saif looked at her just a moment longer.

'No,' he said. 'Not all the people.'

Chapter 24

The nights had got longer. It barely felt like evening as Flora and Lorna got ready. Angus was still sleepy.

'Are you sure he's okay?' Flora had asked, giving him a slightly worried glance. Lorna had shaken her head and pointed out that this was much better than when he'd been in pain and grumpy during the treatment. This was totally to be expected in fact, and she was glad he seemed so much calmer.

Lorna grasped his hand as they left, and promised to bring him back some whisky if she won the raffle. (Every time they got to the raffle too late, and nobody ever remembered who had won or could find their tickets anyway.) Mrs Laird had come to sit with Angus, even though he'd said loudly that he didn't need a babysitter. For God's sake, he wasn't a wee one.

'How are things up at Dr Handsome's?' Flora had asked impishly, glancing at Lorna. Mrs Laird didn't notice.

'Oh, fine, fine,' she said. Then she sniffed. 'He's very tidy,' she said. 'Mostly. Except with the paperwork. Paperwork everywhere!'

'What, like medical notes and things?' said Flora, slightly outraged.

'Oh no, no. That stays in the surgery. No. I can't read it. It's in a funny script.'

'Arabic,' said Flora, nodding.

'FLORA!' said Lorna. 'Stop being a nosy parker!'

'I'm not being nosy! None of us can read Arabic!'

'It comes in from all over,' said Mrs Laird. 'Piles of it.'

They looked at each other.

'I'm not allowed to dust anywhere near it.'

Lorna thought of a different world, a country left behind and all that meant. An entire life shrunk to mounds of government paperwork. They had never discussed it. Not once.

She looked at her father.

'Is he all right?' said Mrs Laird. Angus was snoozing in front of the racing.

'He'll be fine,' said Lorna. 'Give him these' – she pointed to the various pills she'd laid out – 'at ten p.m. And don't let him have any more whisky.'

Angus snorted in his sleep and woke up briefly.

'I mean it.'

'Where are you going?' he said.

'Nowhere,' said Lorna immediately. 'If you want me to stay here.'

He blinked, then shook his head, as if suddenly confused.

'Oh no, love.' He half smiled. 'You know, you look a lot like your mother in that dress. When she was young, I mean, a long time back now. But she was ... she was lovely.'

Lorna came closer.

'I know. Look, I don't need to go out. Why don't I just stay?'

He waved her away.

'Don't be daft. I'm absolutely fine. You're in with me far too much. Everybody knows that. I want you to have a little fun. Go find yourself a nice lad, would you? I'm bored of you cluttering the place up.' And he smiled, so she knew he was joking.

Mrs Laird nodded.

'Go and have a good time. We'll be fine,' she said, as Angus nodded, then seemed to be settling himself down for sleep again. She clasped Lorna's arm, briefly. 'You deserve it.'

At the hotel on the dockside people were already spilling out into the cobbled streets. Usually they had to hold the dance in the function suite because of the weather, but tonight they'd taken over the large back garden. There was a marquee for bars and tables. The band were playing on a stage underneath a huge blanket of stars; smaller than the stars Saif was used to, but just as bright.

It took the girls half an hour to reach the bar, held up as they were by everyone. People usually bought – and sometimes smuggled – bottles, to save themselves having to fight through the red-faced crush too often. Lorna and Flora chatted, said hello, swapped news. Lorna, as usual, did her best to duck out of the way of the more demanding parents. They were the ones who thought that, on a rare night out, she actually wanted to discuss the talents of their beloved children at length. But otherwise, she looked around happily. This would do, she thought.

Chapter 25

The party was in full swing. The noise was growing louder and louder, and the dancing was getting a little wilder. Lorna moved away from the dance floor to get some air. She was more drunk than she had realised. That was the problem with not going out very much: you got a bit overexcited. She'd been hopping from table to table, with people filling up her glass, and now she was feeling a little peculiar.

To her delight, she suddenly spotted Saif. He'd come! He was wearing a simple blue open-necked shirt and a pair of trousers, which meant he didn't stand out as much as he might have done. He was standing near the bar, chatting awkwardly with Ollie the vet and looking very uncomfortable.

'Hey!' she said, waving madly and dodging Valerie Crewsden, who'd moved up from England to launch an artisan craft business. Valerie had a lot to say about her daughter Cressida. She thought Cressida should be on a

Gifted and Talented programme, despite there being no such thing on Mure.

Lorna strode towards them and kissed Ollie, whom she liked. With Saif she thought about it, then, awkward and slightly blushing, shook hands with him instead. But the look of pleasure on his face couldn't be denied.

'Hello,' he said, smiling at her.

'I'm glad you came,' said Lorna.

'So am I,' said Saif, looking at his feet.

'Drink?' said Ollie.

'Yes please!' replied Lorna. At the same instant Saif said, 'No thanks.' Then, as Ollie and Lorna quickly nodded, he shrugged and added, 'Ah well, you know ... Beirut ...'

Ollie gave Lorna a worried look, but Saif just smiled.

'Actually, I will have a little whisky. With Pepsi, please.'

Ollie shook his head in horror.

'No chance,' he said. 'Not Pepsi. Not in Scotland!'

'I will never understand the ways of your country.'

'You can have some water,' said Ollie. 'On the side.'

Saif and Lorna watched him go, and they both laughed.

'He seems very firm,' said Saif.

'It's a serious business up here,' said Lorna.

'I see that.' He smiled.

'I'm disappointed that there's no kilt,' said Lorna.

'You're going to have to somehow get over that.'

They watched the pink-cheeked dancers for a while. They were twirling faster and more violently. Some of the men were sweating as the fiddles and drums played frantically. There was nothing courtly or elegant about this; it was country dancing at its most basic and energetic. Even to Lorna's eyes it looked quite off-putting.

'Are you going to dance?' she asked anyway.

'No,' said Saif, frowning. 'I . . . I need my hands for work.'

Lorna laughed, as Ollie returned with drinks. And then he got swept up in a wild dance, a Strip the Willow, and vanished into the crowd.

'You're funny,' she said.

Saif shrugged. 'No. I am the miserable doctor with dark skin nobody likes.'

'Everybody would like you,' said Lorna, 'if they got to know you.'

'They don't want to know me,' said Saif. 'They just want antibiotics.'

'Can't they have both?'

97

'Antibiotics are bad for the environment. And I think people aren't sure about me.'

'Let me introduce you to some people.'

He froze.

'Can't we ... Let's just stay here a while.'

Lorna suddenly felt her heart beating strongly in her chest, and her face flushing pink. This was crazy. She felt like an underage teenager trying to get served with alcohol. That never worked on Mure, because everyone knew exactly how old you were and what class you were in in school. You could try and fool the Polish boys who came in the holidays to work, but that rarely worked for long.

Nevertheless, she felt exactly the same, at thirty-one years old: sick, giddy, as if her stomach was churning like a washing machine. Surely it must be obvious. She shrank against the side of the marquee, but if anything that made her feel even more on show.

Neither of them could speak.

She gratefully let herself be grabbed away to dance by a large group that needed an extra girl.

'Come with!' she said, tipsy and laughing, but Saif stood there frowning, and shook his head. She was hurled into the excited crowd, tossed around, laughing, twirling, but aware as she danced of his eyes on her. Not intense, not gazing. Just watchful, that was all. And she felt the colour come back into her face even stronger than before.

After the dance, she headed back to the bar – and more wine was drunk. The crush was so heavy now that she couldn't see Saif through the crowd. Then the music changed. The band, who had also been cheerfully drinking a beer or two, had stopped playing Scottish dance music. They were now playing wedding favourites, which meant, Lorna realised, it must be far later than she'd thought.

Sure enough a conga started snaking its way through the garden. She rolled her eyes and disappeared to the loo with Flora, who was very drunk and giggling madly about something that seemed terribly important at the time but that she couldn't remember later. Lorna did remember that they were queuing for the loos and suddenly Flora said, out of the blue, 'So, are you going to go for it or what?'

Lorna looked at her.

'What do you mean?' she said, although she knew exactly what she meant.

'He hasn't taken his eyes off you all evening. You know that. You've been the same, you moony old cow. So. Are you going to go for it?'

'Is everyone talking about this?'

'No,' lied Flora. 'Just me, as I have stunning powers of awareness. And also you talk about him non-bloody-stop.'

'I do not. Do I?'

Flora nodded, her eyes slightly unfocused for a minute. 'So. I mean. Tonight's the night, isn't it?'

'Aren't you on the pull too?'

'Not having much luck,' said Flora. 'That's why I want one of us to be successful.'

'Oh, I don't know,' said Lorna. Though she had that fizzy, excited feeling inside her again just thinking of those eyelashes, so long they nearly brushed his cheekbones; his beautiful skin; the thick dark hair she longed to run her hands through.

'Also, think how annoyed everyone else will be if you get him,' goaded Flora, who could be a monkey sometimes.

'That's a terrible reason for trying to pull someone,' said Lorna, laughing.

'Got any better ones?' said Flora, as Lorna bit her lip and caught sight of herself in the mirror. She looked pink, but good with it; glowing. Some fronds of curly hair were tumbling down around her face. Her pretty summer dress was tied at the waist.

Flora handed her a lipstick and sprayed her quickly with scent.

'You're gorgeous,' she said. 'Now hurry up before he's gone.'

'Do you think ...'

'I think,' said Flora, 'at the very least – at the very VERY least – you both deserve some cheering up. Don't you?'

And Lorna blinked several times, giggled once more, and set her face towards the dance floor.

Chapter 26

Shining, Lorna walked towards the garden – only to see no trace of Saif where she'd left him.

She looked around, puzzled, and then was amused to see that the band were, for some reason, playing a Greek wedding dance, the famous one from the film.

And she was even more amused and amazed to see that Saif was right in the middle of it. Many of the men were now unattractively sweat-soaked and had their tops off or unbuttoned fully. Their arms were around each other's necks as they stumbled from side to side.

Saif was not at all sweaty or pink. He was simply stepping smartly from left to right. He was slightly embarrassed but laughing more and more, as the men beside him laughed too and punched him fondly on the shoulder. That, as Lorna knew, meant they were glad he was there.

It was a silly dance that nobody quite knew how to finish. But they carried on as the band played faster and faster. Saif looked no more or less out of place among the kilts than anyone else. Lorna watched and clapped until finally the music stopped and the men landed in a heap on the floor.

As Saif emerged, he saw her there in front of him, clapping and smiling straight at him. He grinned right back and, without even thinking about it, without either of them thinking about it, she held out her hand to him in a courtly dance fashion, and he took it, laughing. The band started to build up to 'Auld Lang Syne'. Last orders at the bar grew more frenzied, and everyone surged past them onto the dance floor. But they, they went the other way. In front of everyone.

Chapter 27

It had grown colder outside now. They were still laughing and a little tipsy, and excited from all the dancing. Lorna found herself – and this was not at all like her – pulling on his hand, behind the marquee. She led him up through the now silent garden of the hotel, its fairy lights sparkling among the trees, the revellers inside, or gone home to bed. The early roses gave out their spring scent along with the perfume of bluebells in the deeper grass. And she led him to the sturdy tree trunk, both of them under a spell, a cloud of summer nights and dancing and laughter and music.

She turned her face towards his, his eyes so dark, hers clear, light pools. She could sense underneath the blue shirt every inch of his body, not touching her, but so close she could smell his sweet lemony scent, and feel the heat of him. Without taking his eyes off her, he lifted a large hand and moved it towards her. And she was aware how much taller than her he was, as he loomed over her, blocking the light from the dance floor. His hand cupped her chin. The breath caught in her throat as she reached up on tiptoes towards him, ever so gently, the two of them breathing together now, slowly closing the gap, and she closed her eyes ...

And nothing happened.

Chapter 28

Lorna opened her eyes. He was standing there staring at her, his face outlined in the fairy lights, his eyes trained on hers.

'I'm sorry,' he said, backing away. 'I'm sorry. I'm so sorry.'

'It's okay,' she said, worried at first that he'd not understood. 'It's okay. I want . . . I would like you to kiss me.'

She wanted him to kiss her more than anything else in the world.

'It's okay,' she repeated, softly, her hand reaching out once again for him, but he did not take it.

He shook his head.

'For me,' he said. 'For me it is not okay. I am sorry. So sorry.' He backed away even further.

'But . . . what's . . .' Lorna felt herself horribly shamed; her throat tightened. 'What's wrong . . . what's wrong with me?' she found herself stuttering.

He stepped towards her, his eyes burning fiercely.

'There is absolutely nothing wrong with you,' he said in an angry voice. 'You are ... you are very beautiful. You are very lovely. But ...' He threw his hands up in despair. 'I am not free. That is all. I am not a free man.'

And he turned, furiously, and stalked away. He didn't look back, or right or left. And his footsteps faded on the cobbles of the windy harbour and he was gone.

Chapter 29

With that sixth sense friends so often have, Flora found her sitting beneath the tree, trying not to cry.

'Come on,' she hissed. 'Quick. Roddy McClafferty's cab's here, but he's passed out in the bogs. We'll nick it and send it back for him, but you'll have to be quick before anyone else realises.'

. This struck Lorna as a good idea, and they dashed out to Wullie's ancient estate car. It served as a taxi on busy nights, although it smelled of all of his nine dogs at once and still had his ladder in it.

Flora had Lorna's handbag too. Lorna took it weakly.

'How did you know?'

'I saw him stalking off. Snooty, grumpy old bastard,' said Flora. 'I never liked him.'

'Half an hour ago you told me to get off with him!'

'Yes, well, I was younger then.'

Lorna dissolved in tears.

'What's the matter? Was it a religious thing? Or do you have like three tits and you've just never mentioned it?'

The jokes weren't helping. Lorna carried on sobbing.

'No. No. There's ... there's someone else. I think he's married or something.'

'He wasn't wearing a ring.'

'Maybe ... maybe he lost it. Or sold it.'

They thought about that.

'Well, why's he been flirting with you then?' said Flora.

'I don't think he has,' said Lorna. 'I think ... I mean, he doesn't know anyone here. I'm his only friend. I think maybe I misread things ...'

Flora gave her a long look in the light of the harbour street lamps.

'That's odd, because he looked to me like a devoted puppy dog.'

Lorna started to cry again.

'Oh God, now I've messed everything up.'

'You're right,' said Flora. 'Because nobody else has ever had a drunken snog they've regretted later. Nobody ever in the history of the world.' She patted her gently on the shoulder.

'He WALKED OFF,' said Lorna. 'He went to kiss

me and then . . . he just walked off! Left me high and dry! I felt like total shit.'

'That's why I never liked him.'

'Oh God.' Lorna covered her face with her hands. 'What am I going to do next time I need a smear test? I'm going to die of cancer and it will all be his fault.'

'The good thing about you is the way you don't build things up too much in your head,' said Flora.

She gave Lorna a huge hug.

'Listen. It's fine. It'll be okay. Just ignore it. That's what a bloke would do. Pretend it never happened. Ever. He'll do his two years here, then he'll be gone.'

'So I just have to live on a tiny island totally avoiding somebody for two whole years?'

'You can do anything you need to.'

'At least nobody saw us,' said Lorna. 'At least there's that.'

'Did you kiss that doctor?' came Wullie's voice from the front of the car. 'Well, you want to be careful, young lady. People will talk.'

Lorna buried her face in her hands again. Flora rolled her eyes.

Chapter 30

'Okay, I'm ready,' said Lorna in a small voice.

'Are you sure?' said Flora.

'Yes.'

'You're absolutely ready?'

'I am.'

'Ready to look at your phone?'

'I am ready to look at my phone. Pass it over.'

Sure enough, there was a long list of excited questions from people who'd obviously seen them on the dance floor. Plus a tagged picture, which luckily was just of the dance floor. But seriously: already? They were still in Wullie's taxi.

As Lorna was deleting them, the phone rang suddenly, startling them both.

'He is SO sorry,' said Flora. 'But don't go over there.'

'It's not a booty call,' said Lorna. 'He wouldn't send me a booty call.'

'I'm just saying. Don't go over there.'

'I'm not—' Lorna noticed the caller's name.

'Mrs Laird? Hello. Hello? Is everything all right? . . . WHAT?'

Wullie, who had been going to drop Flora off first, made an immediate U-turn.

Chapter 31

Lorna charged into the little cottage, her dress still dancing out behind her.

'Where is he?'

He wasn't responding or moving. Mrs Laird had gone in to check on him at ten, when he was asleep. And at eleven, when he'd seemed a little paler but fine. At midnight she'd got frightened. She'd tried to wake him but couldn't.

His skin was a ghastly grey under the overhead light. Flora was already on her phone.

'Dr MacAllister is on call tonight, and he's on the other side of the island. Do you think we need the air ambulance?'

Lorna just stared at her.

'Yeah. Yeah, of course.'

Flora hung up and dialled 999, and blurted out what was going on.

Meanwhile, Lorna tried to make her father comfortable. He was breathing, just, but it was rattling in and out. She put him in the recovery position, but his skin was clammy. His heartbeat, to her shaking, sweaty fingers, seemed to skitter and jump. She picked up her own phone. With slippery hands, after a couple of failed attempts, she managed to call the very last number she felt like dialling.

Saif wasn't asleep.

In fact, he was crying. For the first time in his adult life.

The girl; the garden; the island. One gentle hand, one near kiss ...

It was as if something had burst inside him. A wall had crumbled, and just as he had feared, once he had started, he didn't know if he could stop. Thank God Mrs Laird wasn't there. He stared at the four walls and just let the tears fall. He let them flow through him like blood pouring from a wound, as if they would never end.

It took him a while to steel himself to pick up the phone. When he saw who it was, he drew his hand back.

'Oh God!' screamed Lorna. 'He won't pick up. You'll have to call him.'

It was a panic out of her worst nightmares, as Flora fiddled with the phone and finally got through to him.

*

When he heard what was happening, Saif swore with startling force and sprinted out of the door, frantically wiping his face with the back of his hand.

Chapter 32

The air ambulance took forever to arrive. The sound of its blades could be heard from a great distance. It was the longest wait of Lorna's life, though she couldn't have said afterwards precisely how long it took. Every moment felt like an hour.

She and Saif hadn't spoken to one another since he'd knocked and slipped in through the door with his large leather bag. He'd immediately knelt down next to her father. He'd peppered Mrs Laird with questions and had set up an IV drip. He worked briskly and calmly, but nothing he did seemed to affect Angus's irregular breathing and his ghastly grey skin.

None the less, the air ambulance crew praised him. Then they turned to Lorna and gestured her into the helicopter.

'I will come,' said Saif straight away.

'Sorry, mate, no room,' said the medic. 'Only space for one.'

Saif nodded. Then he looked directly at Lorna,

who blushed instinctively. She wanted to look away, but forced herself not to.

'I am so sorry,' he said fiercely as she finally steeled herself to meet his gaze. 'I should have picked up the phone. I am ... About everything. I am.'

She shook her head.

'You weren't on call. It wasn't your fault.'

He raised his hands and said something over the noise of the helicopter blades whipping round. But she didn't catch what it was as the chopper lifted into the sky, which was already growing light, and set out over the stormy sea.

Chapter 33

It was like the jumble of a disturbed dream: a night of shouting, of running, and confusion, and consent forms. And the work was done by incredibly clever young people who looked about the age of the schoolchildren she was sending off to secondary school on the mainland.

There were IVs, injections, lines. Her brother Iain burst through off his flight, his face drawn. Then he half smiled and told her she smelled of booze. And he punched her arm and they hugged for a long time.

But then they had a long, long wait as her father was wheeled into surgery. They held hands. Lorna ignored her phone, which pinged and lit up every second. She didn't want to read whatever people had to say. She couldn't bear the idea that it might make it a reality.

It was 5 a.m. when they saw a young, tired figure coming towards them from the end of a long corridor filled with grey light. It was the surgeon. Iain frowned. They'd been told the operation would take far longer.

Lorna froze, watching her taking step after step towards them, a walk she must be dreading. She held her breath. She and Iain clutched each other tightly, unable to look at one another.

The doctor saw them, and took a deep breath of her own.

'I'm so sorry,' she said as she approached, her face drawn with tiredness. 'We tried. But as soon as we opened him up ... The tumour had metastasised ... wrapped around the central cortex. I really am sorry. There was absolutely nothing to be done.'

She blinked.

'Would you like to sit down?'

Even though there was no one else in the waiting area they were in, they followed her blindly into a bland little room with pictures of flowers on the walls and cushions on the chairs.

'I'm afraid he couldn't take the anaesthetic. Opening him up ... It was very much a last-ditch attempt at what we were trying to do.'

Lorna could hear the words, but she didn't understand what they meant.

The doctor was shaking her head.

'We couldn't save him.'

'So what does that mean?' said Lorna.

Iain reached out and put an arm around her. 'He's dead, Loz,' he said gently. 'Dad's dead.'

'But he had the operation,' said Lorna, still confused. They were in the hospital, after all.

'Lorna,' said Iain.

And then she understood.

Chapter 34

Lorna ran blindly out of the hospital, Iain calling her name. She was lucky there was no one about at that time of day. She could barely see through her tears as she charged across roads and along the jetty and caught the very first ferry of the morning.

There was nobody else on board that early. She paced up and down the deck as the waves rose and fell behind her. She was completely unable to think, to deal with the fact that her father was gone.

She finally answered the constant ringing of her phone.

'Where are you?' said Iain.

'I'm heading back.'

'Why?' he said. 'There's stuff to do here, Lorna.'

'What stuff?'

'Well, they'll need to take him away, all that kind of thing, paperwork. If you want to see him ...'

She let out a terrified sob.

'Already?'

There was a pause.

'I don't want to see him,' she said. 'I saw Mum. It didn't help at all. I want to remember him ... the way I loved him.'

There was another pause.

'Okay,' said Iain. 'Well. You do what you want to do.'

Lorna shook her head. She didn't even know where she was going.

'I'll wait for you at home,' she said.

She stared out at the bright horizon, at this ridiculous dawning of a day that didn't have her father in it. Her head hurt, and she was thirsty. Just as she thought this, the kind captain with the thick beard was at her elbow. He held out a huge enamel mug of tea.

'You looked like you needed this,' he said gruffly, then turned away. Lorna stared after him. She took a sip and was very grateful.

'At Dad's?' said Iain.

'Of course. I've been living there.'

There was a long pause then.

'I'm sorry,' said Iain. 'You've done this all by yourself. I didn't realise how serious it was. It's been so hard to get away. I'm sorry, Lorna.'

'It's all right.'

His voice went high and strange. 'I wish I'd had the chance ... I wish I'd been able to say goodbye.'

'He'd have told you to sod off,' said Lorna, smiling through her tears. 'You know he would. Honestly, Iain. He was on the mend. He was quite happy.'

'Just unlucky, that was all.'

There was silence as the ferry droned on across the waves, the sunlight bouncing off them.

'You stay at Dad's,' said Iain finally. 'I'll be there as soon as I can.'

Chapter 35

As she got off the boat, the captain told her to look after herself. Then she found she simply couldn't go back to the farmhouse. Her feet wouldn't let her do it. Not when there would be bowls and plates in the dishwasher, and his clothes in the laundry. His old coat would be hanging on the back of the door, and the fire probably still burning low in the grate.

Instead, she turned back towards the shore. Her tired, so tired, feet were taking her that way. On the beach, she took off her shoes and socks, and let the cold sand squish between her toes.

She wandered up to the headland, then sat down, hugging her knees. She was freezing, but she didn't care. She had so much to do, so much to arrange. There was so much life going on around her. Just a little longer, she thought, and then I will get up. And I know, the one thing I know is that everyone here on Mure, my home, everyone will help me get through this.

They would all pull together – Iain and Mrs

Laird and Flora and Jeannie and Dr MacAllister and the teachers and the children. Everyone helped each other when you lived somewhere like this, and whatever else had happened, it would be a comfort, a definite comfort. She would feel better. One day.

The sky was almost fully light now. The first beams of what promised to be another shining day were creeping over the distant mainland. The ships were passing back and forth in the bay. The lights across the harbour were starting to blink out one by one.

It was a day without her father in it. As bad a dawn as you could get. Her eyes were too tired to cry.

Suddenly she felt a coat over her shoulders. She started, and looked up.

Saif was standing there, not looking at her.

'I'm sorry . . .' she began, but he shook his head curtly and sat down beside her; not right beside her; a little way away.

He too stared into the crashing white surf, and across to the lights popping out on the mainland as another day began. And he looked beyond, too. Beyond the bay and the inlets and the channel and the landlocked sea to oh so very far away.

'There are things . . .' he began, then stopped

125

talking. Now he did move a little closer. Lorna realised she was shaking, but he laid a hand briefly, gently on her arm.

'There are things,' he tried again, and he sounded as if he had something in his throat. 'Things that happen. Even when you think you are safe. There is nowhere safe if you love people, Lorna. I think that is just what being a grown-up is.'

There was a pause, and suddenly Lorna felt her eyes loosening; tears gathering.

'I don't know anything else apart from that.'

'Except you carry on,' said Lorna.

Saif nodded. 'Of course you carry on. There is despair and there is hope.'

Lorna shook her head. 'There is no hope for me.'

Saif tutted crossly. 'You have an entire, safe, loving community here full of children who love you and friends who help you and people who wish you well. And yes, this is so sad, but listen to me. It happened in the right order.'

There was a long pause.

'So,' he said at last. 'Don't you dare tell me you have no hope.'

Lorna let out a loud sob.

He turned his head immediately. 'Sorry,' he said. 'That was far too harsh for today.' He threw

126

a pebble far into the surf. 'I can't ... I never get things right here.'

Lorna nodded. 'It bloody was,' she said. Tears were dripping down her nose. He felt in his pocket and pulled out a large clean handkerchief, like a magician, and she almost smiled as he handed it over.

She trumpeted into it in a not very attractive manner.

'I don't need it back,' he said gravely, and she almost smiled again, through the tears now flowing freely down her cheeks.

'Good,' she said.

They stared out to sea. Another ferry was starting to make its passage across the firth, sunlight glinting off its windows.

'Will you ever give up hope?' she said quietly to Saif, who was watching the movement of the ferry.

'Yes,' he said. 'One day. But not today.'

Chapter 36

Presently Saif looked at her.

'There is a lot to do,' he said.

'I know,' she replied. 'My brother's coming and I suppose everyone will, and there'll be so much to organise ...'

'I can help.'

Lorna stood up and handed him back his jacket. She shook her head.

'No,' she said. 'I can do it.'

'Yes. Of course you can.'

She nodded. Then she turned in the watery early-morning northern light, so cool and clear, even as the sun spread across the stunning glens. A lone kestrel was circling somewhere far away, hooting on the morning breeze.

Saif watched her as she steadily made her way across the dunes to face her new world alone. He watched as she walked along the bumpy track all the way up from the beach towards the quiet road, with its puttering tractors and small horses and stony headlands and wide fields of bracken. He watched until she disappeared from sight. Then he turned his face once more to the incoming tide that washed up on every shore with good news and with bad.

And then he jumped up and ran and shouted her name, and called on her to wait. When he finally caught up with her, panting, she looked confused and a little worried.

'No, please,' he said. 'Let me come. As a friend. Please. Can I . . . can I be with you as a friend?'

When they reached the farmhouse, they found, before they even got to the end of the road, that everyone was already there: Jeannie, all the neighbours, Mrs Laird, Flora, of course, parents from the school, Ewan, Wullie, all of Angus's farmhands, standing by. As they surged forward to meet her, to carry her home, Lorna stopped still and let herself be engulfed by the wave of people as it ebbed and flowed – and Saif joined the wave too, of her life and family and community, and was absorbed. And had you been looking, you would not have noticed any difference between them at all.

About Quick Reads

Quick Reads are brilliant short new books written by bestselling writers. They are perfect for regular readers wanting a fast and satisfying read, but they are also ideal for adults who are discovering reading for pleasure for the first time.

Since Quick Reads was founded in 2006, over 4.5 million copies of more than a hundred titles have been sold or distributed. Quick Reads are available in paperback, in ebook and from your local library.

To find out more about Quick Reads titles, visit
www.readingagency.org.uk/quickreads
Tweet us 🐦 @Quick_Reads

Quick Reads is part of The Reading Agency,
a national charity that inspires more people to read more, encourages them to share their enjoyment of reading with others and celebrates the difference that reading makes to all our lives.
www.readingagency.org.uk Tweet us @readingagency

The Reading Agency Ltd · Registered number: 3904882 (England & Wales) Registered charity number: 1085443 (England & Wales) Registered Office: Free Word Centre, 60 Farringdon Road, London, EC1R 3GA The Reading Agency is supported using public funding by Arts Council England.

We would like to thank all our funders:

LOTTERY FUNDED

Quick Reads has something for everyone

Stories to make you laugh

DEAD MAN Talking
RODDY DOYLE

Two women, one man...
RED FOR REVENGE
Fanny Blake

Rules for *Dating a* Romantic Hero
Harriet Evans

JOJO MOYES
Paris for ~~Two~~ One

A BABY AT THE BEACH CAFÉ
Lucy Diamond

EDITED BY VERONICA HENRY
ANNIVERSARY
Ten tempting stories from ten bestselling authors

Stories to make you feel good

Stories to take you to another place

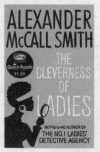

ALEXANDER McCALL SMITH
THE CLEVERNESS OF LADIES
BESTSELLING AUTHOR OF THE NO.1 LADIES' DETECTIVE AGENCY

DOCTOR WHO
THE SILURIAN GIFT
Mike Tucker

Stories about real life

Stories to take you to another time

Stories to make you turn the pages

For a complete list of titles visit

www.readingagency.org.uk/quickreads

Available in paperback, ebook and from your local library

Discover the pleasure of reading with Galaxy®

Curled up on the sofa,
Sunday morning in pyjamas,
just before bed,
in the bath or
on the way to work?

Wherever, whenever,
you can escape
with a good book!

So go on...
indulge yourself with
a good read and the
**smooth taste of
Galaxy® chocolate.**

Proudly
supports

Why not start a reading group?

If you have enjoyed this book, why not share your next Quick Read with friends, colleagues, or neighbours?

The Reading Agency also runs **Reading Groups for Everyone** which helps you discover and share new books. Find a reading group near you, or register a group you already belong to and get free books and offers from publishers at **readinggroups.org**

There is a free toolkit with lots of ideas to help you run a Quick Reads reading group at **www.readingagency.org.uk/quickreads**

Share your experiences of your group on Twitter

🐦 @Quick_Reads

Continuing your reading journey

As well as Quick Reads, The Reading Agency runs lots of programmes to help keep you and your family reading.

Reading Ahead invites you to pick six reads and record your reading in a diary to get a certificate **readingahead.org.uk**

World Book Night is an annual celebration of reading and books on 23 April **worldbooknight.org**

Chatterbooks children's reading groups and the **Summer Reading Challenge** inspire children to read more and share the books they love **readingagency.org.uk/children**

Life on Mure island continues in
The Summer Seaside Kitchen – read on
for the beginning!

The Summer Seaside Kitchen
by
Jenny Colgan

Flora is definitely, absolutely sure that escaping
from the quiet Scottish island where she grew up
to the noise and hustle of the big city was the right
choice. What was there for her on Mure? It's a place
where everyone has known her all her life, and no
one will let her forget the past. In the city, she can
be anonymous, ambitious and indulge herself in
her hopeless crush on her gorgeous boss, Joel.

When a new client demands Flora's
presence back on Mure, she's suddenly swept back
into life with her brothers (all strapping, loud
and seemingly incapable of basic housework) and
her father. As Flora indulges her new-found love
of cooking and breathes life into the dusty little
pink-fronted shop on the harbour, she's also going
to have to come to terms with past mistakes – and
work out exactly *where* her future lies ...

Hiraeth (n): *a homesickness for a home to which you can not return, a home which maybe never was; the nostalgia, the yearning, the grief for lost places in your past.*

Chapter One

If you have ever flown into London – I did originally type 'You know when you fly into London?' and then I thought, well, that might be a bit presumptuous, like hey-ho, here I am flying about all the time, whereas the reality is I've always bought the cheapie discount flight that meant I had to get up at 4.30 a.m. and therefore didn't sleep at all the night before in case I missed the alarm and actually it ended up costing me more to get to the airport at an ungodly hour and then pour overpriced coffee down myself than it would have done just to buy a sensibly timed flight in the first place ... but anyway.

So.

If you've ever flown into London, you'll know that they often have to put you in a holding pattern, where you circle about, waiting for a landing slot. And I never usually mind it; I like seeing the vast expanse of the huge city below me, that unfathomable number of people busying away, the idea that every single one of them is full of hopes and dreams and disappointments, street after street after street, millions and millions of souls and dreams. I always find it pleasingly mind-boggling.

And if you had been hovering over London on this particular day in early spring, then beneath you you would have seen the massive, endless sprawl; the surprising amount of green space clustered in the west, where it looks as if you could walk clear across the city through its parks, and on to the clustered, smoky east, the streets and spaces becoming ever more congested; the wheel along the river glinting in the early-morning sun, the ships moving up and down the sometimes dirty, sometimes gleaming water, and the great glass towers that seem to have sprung up without anyone asking for them as London changes in front of your eyes; past the Millennium Dome, getting lower now, and there's the shining point of Canary Wharf, once the highest skyscraper in the country, with its train station that stops in the middle of the building, something that must have seemed pretty awesome in about 1988.

But let's imagine you could carry on; could zoom down like a living Google Maps in which you don't only go and look at your own house (or that might just be me).

If you carry on down further, it would pretty soon stop looking so serene, less as if you were surveying it like a god in the sky, and you'd start to notice how crowded everything is and how grubby it all looks, and how many people are shoving past each other, even now, when it's not long past 7 a.m., exhausted-looking cleaners who've just finished their dawn shifts trudging home in the opposite direction to the eager suited and booted young men and women; office jockeys and retail staff and mobile phone fixers and Uber drivers and window cleaners and *Big Issue* sellers and the many, many men wearing hi-vis vests who do mysterious things with traffic cones; and we're nearly at ground level now, whizzing round corners, following the path of the Docklands Light Railway, with its passengers trying to hold their own against the early-morning crush, because there is no way around it, you have to stick your elbows out, otherwise you won't get a place, might not even get to stand: the idea of possibly getting a seat stops miles back at Gallions Reach, but you might, you might just get a corner place to stand that isn't pressed up against somebody's armpit, the carriage thick with coffee and hungover breath and halitosis and the sense that everyone has been somehow ripped from their beds too soon, that even the watery sunlight tilting over the horizon in this early spring isn't entirely convinced about it; but tough, because the great machine of London is all ready and waiting, hungry, always hungry, to swallow you up, squeeze everything it can out of you and send you back to do the entire thing in reverse.

And there is Flora MacKenzie, with her elbows out, waiting to get on the little driverless train that will take her into the absurd spaghetti chaos of Bank station. You can see her: she's just stepping on. Her hair is a strange colour; very, very pale. Not blonde, and not red exactly, and kind of possibly strawberry blonde, but more faded than that. It's almost not a colour at all. And she is ever so slightly too tall; and her skin is pale as milk and her eyes are a watery colour and it's sometimes quite difficult to tell exactly what colour they are. And there she is, her bag and her briefcase tight by her side, wearing a mac that she's not sure is too light or too heavy for the day.

141

At this moment in time, and still pretty early in the morning, Flora MacKenzie isn't thinking about whether she's happy or sad, although that is shortly going to become very, very important.

If you could have stopped and asked her how she was feeling right at that moment, she'd probably have just said, 'Tired.' Because that's what people in London are. They're exhausted or knackered or absolutely frantic all the time because . . . well, nobody's sure why, it just seems to be the law, along with walking quickly and queuing outside pop-up restaurants and never, ever going to Madame Tussauds.

She's thinking about whether she will be able to get into a position where she can read her book; about whether the waistband on her skirt has become tighter, while simultaneously and regretfully thinking that if that thought ever occurs to you, it almost certainly has; about whether the weather is going to get hotter, and if so, is she going to go bare-legged (this is problematic for many reasons, not least because Flora's skin is paler than milk and resists any attempts to rectify this. She tried fake tan, but it looked as if she'd waded into a paddling pool full of Bisto. And as soon as she started walking, the backs of her knees got sweaty – she hadn't even known the backs of your knees *could* get sweaty – and long dribbling white lines cut through the tan, as her office mate Kai kindly pointed out to her. Kai has the most creamy coffee-coloured skin and Flora envies it very much. She also prefers autumn in London, on the whole).

She is thinking about the Tinder date she had the other night, where the guy who had seemed so nice online immediately started making fun of her accent,

142

as everybody does, everywhere, all the time; then, when he saw this wasn't impressing her, suggested they skip dinner and just go back to his house, and this is making her sigh.

She's twenty-six, and had a lovely party to prove it, and everyone got drunk and said that she was going to find a boyfriend any day, or, alternately, how it was that in London it was just impossible to meet anyone nice; there weren't any men and the ones there were were gay or married or evil, and in fact not everyone got drunk because one of her friends was pregnant for the first time and kept making a massive deal out of it while pretending not to and being secretly delighted. Flora was pleased for her, of course she was. She doesn't want to be pregnant. But even so.

Flora is squashed up against a man in a smart suit. She glances up, briefly, just in case, which is ridiculous: she's never seen *him* get the DLR; *he* always arrives looking absolutely spotless and uncreased and she knows he lives in town somewhere.

As usual, at her birthday party, Flora's friends knew better than to ask her about her boss after she'd had a couple of glasses of Prosecco. The boss on whom she has the most ridiculous, pointless crush.

If you have ever had an utterly agonising crush, you will know what this is like. Kai knows exactly how pointless this crush is, because he works for him too, and can see their boss clearly for exactly what he is, which is a terrible bastard. But there is of course no point telling this to Flora.

Anyway, the man on the train is not him. Flora feels stupid for looking. She feels fourteen whenever she so much as thinks about him, and her pale cheeks don't

143

hide her blushes at all. She knows it's ridiculous and stupid and pointless. She still can't help it.

She starts half reading her book on her Kindle, crammed in the tiny carriage, trying not to swing into anyone; half looking out of the window, dreaming. Other things bubbling in her mind:

a) She's getting another new flatmate. People move so often in and out of her big Victorian flatshare, she rarely gets to know any of them. Their old mail piles up in the hallway amid the skeletons of dead bicycles, and she thinks someone should do something about it, but she doesn't do anything about it.

b) Whether she should move again.

c) Boyfriend. Sigh.

d) Time for Pret A Manger?

e) Maybe a new hair colour? Something she could remove? Would that shiny grey suit her, or would she look like she had grey hair?

f) Life, the future, everything.

g) Whether to paint her room the same colour as her new hair, or whether that would mean she had to move too.

h) Happiness and stuff.

i) Cuticles.

j) Maybe not silver, maybe blue? Maybe a bit blue? Would that be okay in the office? Could she buy a blue bit and put it in, then take it out?

k) Cat?

And she's on her way to work, as a paralegal, in the centre of London, and she isn't happy particularly,

144

but she isn't sad because, Flora thinks, this is just what everyone does, isn't it? Cram themselves on to a commute. Eat too much cake when it's someone's birthday in the office. Vow to go to the gym at lunchtime but don't make it. Stare at a screen for so long they get a headache. Order too much from ASOS then forget to send it back.

Sometimes she goes from tube to house to office without even noticing what the weather is doing. It's just a normal, tedious day.

Although in two hours and forty-five minutes, it won't be.

Jenny COLGAN'S

BOOKS FOR CHILDREN

Polly is waiting for something important to happen.

But waiting is hard. Can Polly find enough to do to keep busy ALL day? And what will happen when her puffin friend, Neil, decides to fly off into a storm?

Jenny Colgan's debut novel for young readers!

When Polly discovers an injured puffin, she and her mummy look after him in their cottage by the sea. Slowly, Neil's wing heals and Polly must prepare herself to say goodbye to her new friend. Will she ever see him again?

Beautifully illustrated by Thomas Docherty

'Gorgeous, glorious, uplifting'
MARIAN KEYES

Can baking mend a broken heart?

Polly Waterford is recovering from a toxic relationship. Unable to afford their flat, she has to move to a quiet seaside resort in Cornwall, where she lives alone. And so Polly takes out her frustrations on her favourite hobby: making bread. With nuts and seeds, olives and chorizo, and with reserves of determination Polly never knew she had, she bakes and bakes and bakes. And people start to hear about it ...

Is Polly about to lose everything she loves?

Summer has arrived in the Cornish town of Mount Polbearne and Polly Waterford couldn't be happier. Because Polly is in love. And yet there's something unsettling about the gentle summer breeze that's floating through town. Polly sifts flour, kneads dough and bakes bread, but nothing can calm the storm she knows is coming: Is Polly about to lose everything she loves?

Meet Issy Randall, proud owner of *The Cupcake Café*

After a childhood spent in her beloved Grampa Joe's bakery, Issy Randall has undoubtedly inherited his talent so when she's made redundant from her job, Issy decides to seize the moment. Armed with recipes from Grampa, The Cupcake Café opens its doors. But Issy has absolutely no idea what she's let herself in for . . .

One way or another, Issy is determined to have a merry Christmas!

Issy Randall is in love and couldn't be happier. Her new business is thriving and she is surrounded by close friends. But when her boyfriend is scouted for a possible move to New York, Issy is forced to face up to the prospect of a long-distance romance, and she must decide what she holds most dear.

Remember the rustle of the pink and green striped paper bag?

Rosie Hopkins thinks leaving her busy London life, and her boyfriend Gerard, to sort out her elderly Aunt Lilian's sweetshop in a small country village is going to be dull. Boy, is she wrong. Lilian Hopkins has spent her life running Lipton's sweetshop, through wartime and family feuds. As she struggles with the idea that it might finally be time to settle up, she also wrestles with the secret history hidden behind the jars of beautifully coloured sweets.

Curl up with Rosie, her friends and her family as they prepare for a very special Christmas...

Rosie is looking forward to Christmas. Her sweetshop is festooned with striped candy canes, large tempting piles of Turkish Delight, crinkling selection boxes and happy, sticky children. She's going to be spending it with her boyfriend, Stephen, and her family, flying in from Australia. She can't wait. But when a tragedy strikes at the heart of their little community, all of Rosie's plans are blown apart. Is what's best for the sweetshop also what's best for Rosie?

'A fun, warm-hearted read'
WOMAN & HOME

There's more than one surprise in store for Rosie Hopkins this Christmas ...

Rosie Hopkins, newly engaged, is looking forward to an exciting year in the little sweetshop she owns and runs. But when fate strikes Rosie and her boyfriend, Stephen, a terrible blow, threatening everything they hold dear, it's going to take all their strength and the support of their families and their Lipton friends to hold them together.

After all, don't they say it takes a village to raise a child?

Life is sweet!

As the cobbled alleyways of Paris come to life, Anna Trent is already at work, mixing and stirring the finest chocolate. It's a huge shift from the chocolate factory she used to work in back home until an accident changed everything. With old wounds about to be uncovered and healed, Anna is set to discover more about real chocolate – and herself – than she ever dreamed.

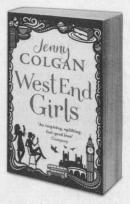

The streets of London are the perfect place to discover your dreams...

When, out of the blue, twin sisters Lizzie and Penny learn they have a grandmother living in Chelsea, they are even more surprised when she asks them to flat-sit her King's Road pad while she is in hospital. They jump at the chance to move to London but, as they soon discover, it's not easy to become an It Girl, and west end boys aren't at all like Hugh Grant ...

Sun, sea and laughter abound in this warm, bubbly tale

Evie is desperate for a good holiday with peaceful beaches, glorious sunshine and (fingers crossed) some much-needed sex. So when her employers invite her to attend a conference in the beautiful South of France, she can't believe her luck. At last, the chance to party under the stars with the rich and glamorous, to live life as she'd always dreamt of it. But things don't happen in quite the way Evie imagines ...

How does an It Girl survive when she loses everything?

Sophie Chesterton is a girl about town, but deep down she suspects that her superficial lifestyle doesn't amount to very much. Her father is desperate for her to make her own way in the world, and when after one shocking evening her life is turned upside down, she suddenly has no choice. Barely scraping by, living in a hovel with four smelly boys, eating baked beans from the can, Sophie is desperate to get her life back. But does a girl really need diamonds to be happy?

A feisty, flirty tale of one woman's quest to cure her disastrous love life

Posy is delighted when Matt proposes, but a few days later disaster strikes: he backs out of the engagement. Crushed and humiliated, Posy wonders why her love life has always ended in disaster. Determined to discover how she got to this point, Posy resolves to get online and track down her exes. Can she learn from past mistakes? And what if she has let Mr Right slip through her fingers on the way?

Keep in touch with
Jenny COLGAN

Chat with Jenny and meet her other readers:

[f] /JennyColganBooks   [t] /@jennycolgan

Check out Jenny's website and sign up
to her newsletter for all the latest book news
plus mouth-watering recipes.

www.jennycolgan.com

LOVE TO READ?

Join **The Little Book Café** for competitions,
sneak peeks and more.

[f] /TheLittleBookCafe

[t] /@littlebookcafe